# Sips of Coffee

## A Short Story Collection

## Keelan LaForge

**ISBN:** 9798864535509

# *Note From Author*

I have spent the last few months composing short stories for writing contests and I wanted to compile them into a book. It's designed to pair with a coffee break, so you can read one story while you enjoy and a break and your favourite beverage. I hope you find some truth, enjoyment and inspiration in them.

# Table of Contents

# Street of Sisterhood

Inspired by Reedsy Prompt - Write a story about two friends who find themselves competing for something: a job, a prize, a love interest, etc.

1800+ Creative Writing Prompts To Inspire You Right Now (reedsy.com)

"I'm not competitive."

"Neither am I."

Kaley and Sam thought they knew themselves, but how well did they know each other? They'd been friends for what felt like an age. They'd done everything alongside one another for decades. It wasn't planned, but their lives just seemed to converge time and again, like planes in a coordinated display - but they'd never been the fighter kind, just the friendly kind. Friendship is a tenuous thing. It can all change in a minute over something seemingly innocuous, like something slight that the wind carries in. People believe nothing can tear them apart until they're looking at their own shredded halves of what was once one, shared page.

They thought they'd always be on friendly terms, until the house appeared. They were house hunting in tandem. They both sent each other any promising prospects they found online. They weren't looking for the same thing at all - Kaley wanted something airy and city-based while Sam wanted to be sequestered away in a countryside cottage. It wasn't a rivalry; it was a supportive search shared between friends.

That was why they were surprised by each other at the open viewing. They'd told each other they were both attending one, but neither had dreamt it would be at the same location. They had both fallen in love with the place before they'd even got out of their cars. It was one of those idyllic places that look like they can only exist in airbrushed magazines, but it was real and with an affordable price tag. Kaley gave Sam a strained smile and Sam returned it. They didn't hide how unhappy they were to see each other well at all. They had genuinely always been happy to see each other until that moment. It's funny how one small, added weight can tip the scale in the other direction.

The agent greeted them at the door, while he also greeted all the other viewers. There were so many keen potential bidders; everyone knew their chance of getting the place was as slim as the hallway felt with twenty people crammed into it. Each potential buyer lingered in the rooms, showing how loath they were to leave. It was a competitive atmosphere. One person looked another squarely in the eye, as if to say, are you going to dare outbid me? It wasn't a friendly atmosphere, however friendly the house felt.

Kaley stepped in front of Sam and made her way inside first. Ordinarily, she always would have held the door open and said, "after you." They both basked in the beauty of their new home – the one they would, they realised, lose a friend to get.

After being ejected by the agent whenever he jangled his keys to tell them the viewing time had ended, they left in separate cars without exchanging a word. Kaley went home, where she awaited a message from Sam, offering her the house, but it didn't arrive.

From there, the bidding war commenced. The price kept jumping up, and no one seemed to find its increase unreasonable. They just thought of the pink horse chestnut trees in the garden and the little brook at the end of the lawn. They thought of the sun-filled rooms with the dancing shadows of tree branches that moved on the walls. They thought of the heady scent of roses and the joyous moments they would spend inside its walls. Kaley had always hated expressions like "forever home," but that was what it was to anyone that had the pleasure of viewing it. They both went beyond their budget to outdo each other. Each of them had the estate agent as a regular contact on their phones. They both sought out constant updates on the status of the house sale. But in that whole time, they didn't talk to each other – they didn't even send a single, civil message. The sisterhood they'd spent their lives building had become nothing but a sham. They couldn't bear to face each other, because doing that would be like facing up to their own disappointment, to their own need for acquiescence where the house was concerned. Neither of them was prepared to acquiesce and let the other have it, for the sake of friendship. The place had a personality as strong as a person's. It felt like it would be enough to fill the void left by their dead friendship.

Their phones rang, simultaneously, with two different agents on the ends of the lines. They had both been outbid. The price had skyrocketed to the point that they could no longer match it, never mind outdo it. The professional tones of the agents weren't sympathetic enough to their plight. They had invested their whole hearts in the house, and it was never going to belong to either of them. They didn't know who the highest bidder was, and they didn't know that it wasn't each other. They just knew that their dreams were like mirages that had vanished, shattered like broken shards of mirror on cold, tiled floors.

A month passed by, and they individually drove to the house – an idea at once in their two heads. They pulled up on the opposite side of the street and parked under the draped veiling of the trees. They tried to approach the place, circumspectly, investigating to see who had taken up residence there. Neither of them believed it was right to do that, but they had to know anyway. And so, they ended up standing side by side, on the same side of the street, looking at the occupied house that neither of them owned. Their eyes met at that moment of realisation, as they watched a kid they didn't know playing basketball in the driveway, sinking shots they never could have made. The longer they looked at the house, the more they realised it was never meant to be theirs, to be theirs to fight over. They looked at each other with coy smiles, mirroring each other, and took a simultaneous step towards each other's spot in the sun.

# *Paper Cups and Confetti Dreams*

Set your story at a large entertainment venue, after the show

has ended, amongst the discarded plastic cups and confetti.

1800+ Creative Writing Prompts To Inspire You Right Now (reedsy.com)

"I can still feel it rushing through me."

"Do you need the bathroom?"

"No, I need my next fix."

"What was so spectacular about it?"

"Everything."

"I don't get it."

I was sitting, floored by the concert, in a sea of clutter on the sticky floor. Cups were tossed underfoot with trampled confetti, and we were the only ones still there. The place was eerily quiet after utter chaos that could only be compared to Beatlemania, and I was a front row fan. My heart was racing like I'd had an unnatural high, but it wasn't that; it was the thrill of the gig. And it was over. I'd put all my dreams into it for the last year. I knew it was coming and I couldn't wait, yet I had willed it away because I couldn't cope with it being over. And there I sat on the floor, clutching my crumpled, unsigned poster, still waiting for a scrawl. I knew I was unlikely to get it, but I still couldn't give up hope. I just wished I'd come with someone more enthusiastic than Becki. She wasn't a fan of my music at all. She had endured it for my sake, but only, she'd said, because it was for one night. I'd have to return the favour some time, or she'd never let it go. I was trembling from my long-contained anticipation that had been released in a two-hour burst and left me frail on the floor.

Why did the music inspire such devotion in its fans? Everyone that didn't love it was perplexed by its draw. They thought it was all "samey," or so I'd been told. But to me, it was life-altering. Something is life-altering to everyone, but most people won't understand why the thing you've chosen is life-altering to you. Becki looked bored sitting there on the floor. She had hung around for a long time for someone that had never wanted to be there to begin with, and the bar had closed long ago. It was just us and the litter. It was strange that no one seemed to have noticed we were there. There was no quick clean-up as expected. The place was like an evacuated disaster zone. There was a deserted kind of beauty in it that made it hard to leave. Becki didn't agree. She was on her feet and impatiently tapping one of them. It echoed in the empty concert hall. I knew we were leaving then.

We turned and walked away from the stage, until it became nothing but a distant step. And then, I heard a voice over the speakers. It was in Korean, and I didn't know what was being said, but it didn't matter. I knew it was my favourite band. That was all I had to know. I raced back to the stage.

"See, patience does pay off," I shouted to Becki.

She rolled her eyes at me, but she followed me, with a secret smile.

I couldn't speak any Korean, despite adoring K-Pop. My favourite singers couldn't speak any English either. We were lost in that place where words aren't enough. We could speak without being understood, but it still felt like we weren't missing anything. They smiled at me and nodded appreciatively. I got them to sign everything I had with me. They welcomed me onto the stage, like I was one of them. Looking at the waste in the huge room made me realise what the audience looked like from their perspective. I pretended each empty cup was a person, watching the stage. I didn't know how they had the bravery to do what they did. They were able to be themselves, unapologetically, whether people liked them or not. And it had paid off, because they owned that stage and that crowd. But I was the only straggler; the only one that waited it out, an hour after the show, hoping that I might catch a brief glimpse of them. Waiting in the dust of that concert was worth it after all. You can think you're there for the main event when the lights and noise are at their most heightened, but it's often the quiet aftermath that brings the biggest surprise of all.

I said goodbye to my favourite band, knowing nothing could top that moment. But still, I will go on to try to find something that will. That's what life is all about. Becki did a good job of pretending to be happy to be there, and I'll return the favour when she wants to see her favourite death metal band. As we walked away, they sang us a verse of one of my favourite songs, and I swooned hearing it. People are always describing K-Pop fans as if they're delusional devotees. Maybe we are. I most definitely am, and I'm not afraid to admit it. On the way out of that gig, I was buzzing more than any other time in my life. Becki was probably buzzing with irritation by then, but at least we were both on the same page energy-wise.

We left the concert hall, and I didn't feel the need to longingly turn back for a last look at it. That only happens whenever things feel unfinished. Becki looked at me brightly and she gave me a nudge. "K-Poop isn't so bad after all," she laughed. "At least they have time for their fans."

"I'm sure your favourite band does too."

"Yeah, they just might show it by throwing stuff at us instead, or by spitting into the crowd."

"I'm sure if you got them alone, you'd have a good conversation."

"Is that your way of agreeing to wait to meet mine the next time round?"

"Yeah, of course – I'll be as long suffering as you are," I laughed. "I know I might have to suffer a bit more than you did, but still – "

"You're cheeky – do you know that? What I went through tonight for you. I have a confession to make though.

"What?"

"I don't hate K-Pop anymore."

"Does this mean you'll stop calling it K-Poop?"

# _Typical Jimmy_

## _Shortlisted in the Reedsy Prompts Contest_

Write a story that experiments with tone — perhaps a difficult

subject dealt with in a playful way, or an ostensibly happy

scene that hints at darkness lurking beneath.

1800+ Creative Writing Prompts To Inspire You Right Now (reedsy.com)

He died the other day. It was like his day of birth, but in reverse. Party poppers were pulled. He didn't want his funeral to be anything less than a joy. Everybody he knew was there. They wanted the cocktail sausages on little sticks, and the vol au vents with that mushroom paste that tastes like birth and death in a sauce. The after party was even more fun than the funeral. He got a great send off. He had a lot of friends, and he'd hosted a lot of parties. He used to joke about when he died. He said it would be the cigarettes that killed him, and they did. He asked for party tunes to be played on the day. He had it all worked out so nobody would be sad, and they were – but they didn't show it. It was like a kids' birthday party. They even had a bouncy castle. What a weird day. If funerals were like that, I'd be eager to go to all of them. Why are most of them held in stuffy churches with stiff services? It's like they don't want to make everyone's mourning period worse; not Jimmy - he had a sense of humour about everything.

In the hospital, he didn't like the tubes. He said he only liked to get his fluids in a glass with some rocks. They said everything in his body was failing, as it tends to do when you're on your way out. He just shrugged and laughed it off, making jokes about his organ donation form being rejected. He didn't have anything anyone wanted, he said. People used their bodies while they were alive, but his was like a worn-out, third hand shoe – it had taken so much humorous use and abuse. I visited in the hospital, but only once. He didn't want anyone to come onto the ward. He said it stank of shit and he was surrounded by people that needed their nappies changed. He wasn't quite ready for the new-born stage again. He could turn anything in life into a party, but not on the ward. The nurses tried to liven up the situation and he gave them his usual witty repartee. But there was too much suffering around him. That was the silly fact. He'd be next – unless he could just shake it off like braving a stubbed toe.

When I saw him, he shouted "yeo, what about you?" across the room – the usual Belfast banter. Nobody raised an eyebrow. They must have been used to his volume and enthusiasm by then. He sat with his feet off the bed, like he was ready to run, any minute - not a feeble granny toilet run either; a marathon-worthy sprint to the next county. He told me to sit down and served me some cordial from the overfilled bedside jug. I drank it out of the plastic cup, tasting antiseptic as I did. Whether it was from the cup or coming to my nostrils through the air, I couldn't tell. It just tasted like a hospital drink – an alcohol-free tipple, like I was at a kid's birthday party and someone had dropped something in the juice. I asked Jimmy how he was, and he wafted my comment away.

"Let's talk about something interesting," he said.

"I have to talk about my symptoms every time they come over with their clipboard. Nobody wants to know anything else."

"Do you think you'll get to go home?" I asked him.

"I'll make sure of it," he said. "I'm not expiring in this shithole."

I laughed. Our eyes connected and that familiar twinkle appeared that I knew so well. The party host was still in there. His mind was a million miles ahead of his body, like a motorbike speeding into the distance, leaving a slow driver chugging along far behind. He told me to get out of the place while I could. I had to anyway: the visiting hours were up. They were only an hour long on that ward. They were probably trying not to tire anyone out too much in case they took their final sleep afterwards. By the looks of things, that would have been a favour to most of them.

I left the ward, hearing Jimmy's distinctive cackle behind me. He was probably chatting up the nurses – looking for the next bit of entertainment. That's all life was about to him. When he died a week later, I was shocked. I should have seen it coming, but you can never get ready for something like that. He'd checked himself out of hospital before that. He told them if they didn't remove the tubes, he'd do it himself and it wouldn't be pretty. He said he had to attend to his affairs, which was code for "fuck hospital; I'm going home." A friend found him in his house days later, face down on the floor. He looked unrecognisable; he didn't look like he'd been laughing when it happened.

After the funeral, I got a strange piece of news. He'd left everything to me in his will. His physical possessions didn't amount to much, but he had a hefty sum stored in the bank. That was a surprise to me; I'd always thought he was a spend-as-you-go type of person. Why he left it solely to me, I'll never understand, but I didn't get to jump for joy too soon. I was in mourning, and there was the funeral to attend to. That was the trade off – I got the money, but I had to arrange the whole thing. Still, I was honoured he entrusted it with me. He always said I could throw a party almost as good as his.

Another week passed and I had a knock at the door. I thought it was the postman. I'd ordered a few things I needed, and we always had a yarn at the door when he arrived with the pretty parcels and the bad bills. I was taken aback when I saw who it was. It was a lady I knew that used to hang around Jimmy all the time. He described her as a "funny bird," and she was. She didn't have any social skills, but she insisted on always being there. She'd taken a shine to him, and she never accepted it wasn't mutual. Jimmy could have flirted with a lamppost anyway. His wit didn't mean anything deeper, but she was sure it did. She looked older than us and frail – the type of person that couldn't make two knitting needles work together, but impressions are often wrong. She plunged the knife into my chest, repeatedly and without mercy.

"You took everything of his," she yelled. The usual tremor in her hand and in her voice were gone. She was like a different person.

"You took what he should have left to me."

She stabbed me until the neighbours saw and called emergency services. Thankfully, they weren't too far away. They bundled her into the backseat of their car, locking her in, like a kid that needs child locks on the doors. As the wheeled me into the back of the ambulance on a stretcher, I laughed to myself. The whole situation was just so typically Jimmy.

# A Desert Dream

Write a story about someone undertaking a long, dangerous journey.

1800+ Creative Writing Prompts To Inspire You Right Now (reedsy.com)

Lost in Arizona, on the holiday of my dreams. A five-figure holiday that I saved up for, for years. Down the toilet it went, whenever my girlfriend kicked me out of the car. We had a stupid fight. She was driving, I was swearing. She blamed the heat, I blamed her personality. She kicked me out of the car, in the back end of nowhere. I'd always wanted to visit the desert. It was on my bucket list, long before I met Angel. She and I had become one of those units that goes everywhere as a twosome, whether it's advisable or not. She was more of a Northern Europe type of holiday maker, but she'd agreed to accompany me, to help me achieve my life's dream.

I'd had a crappy job for decades and I'd endured it, in the hopes that it would fund my biggest dream. I was living it, but it wasn't what it had promised. The vast plains were indeed breath-taking, but my breath was taken away with every dreaded step I took, that progressed towards nothing. I didn't know where on Earth I was – literally.

I'd seen all the typical "lost in the desert" stories – dried out mouth, dried up saliva, blurred vision, delusions of recognisable points that are truly only mirages. I'd never thought any of those things would occur on a real-life trip to the desert, but here I was, lost and as dehydrated as a crispy cactus. The cacti I'd waited my entire life to see were becoming like unwanted friends – following me at every turn. Their arms made them look like animated beings to my tired eyes. For moments, I thought they were like cheery men wearing sombreros, welcoming me into native lands, but they were never alive. They were never friends of mine.

There were so many rocky formations, and I'd started to climb one, but I didn't have the right gear, and I didn't know what I was doing. I wanted to see the panoramic view – the kind where you look at the expansive desert below you – just quiet, yellow sand peppered with little green cacti figures, but I hadn't got to see it from above – or from a place of peacefulness. I kept hoping I would reach that place again, but panic was well and truly setting in.

Angel had abandoned me, at the side of a dusty road, and then she'd torn off at a speed I'd never seen her reach before. I'd expected her to come back, after her temper subsided, but she never had. I'd waited for a long time – an eternity in the broiling sun, but I didn't hear an engine, or the rumble of an oncoming car making fresh tracks in the sand. I wished I did – I wished every argument we'd ever had away, even though in my heart, I knew we were completely incompatible. I wanted romance for that moment – for it to whisk me out of the place I worried I would expire in. My carcass would be found, stripped by vultures, months or years later – at this unmarked part of the globe where tombstones and body identification were unhcard of.

My mind flicked backwards, to a small number of months before, like it was skipping chapters of a book – like sections had gone missing with my present-moment thoughts. I couldn't think clearly, and my memories were becoming like crystallised moments of beauty - the last sparkles of dying sunlight. The pictures I'd seen online had looked exactly like what stood before me, but looking at them from a different perspective changed them into an entirely different scene. It had been beautiful then – desirable, an enviable location, when I'd been cooped up in my grey office block, inputting data in black and white. I'd longed for the space provided by the Arizonian desert. I'd heard so many fables about it, but I'd never met someone that had seen it first-hand. My office in Dublin felt so far from it I might as well have been located at a space station beyond the skies. But my desert dream was clear, and the desire for it had haunted me throughout my life. Maybe it was fitting that the same scenery would haunt me until my moment of death.

I'd been walking for so long that I had lost all concept of time. My phone was in my pocket, but it had no signal and then the battery had gone flat. I didn't even have a bottle of water. When I'd got out of the car, I hadn't even had time to grab my wallet – not that it would have done me any good there. There wasn't a building in sight, for tens or maybe even hundreds of miles. The air around me seemed to move, in ripples, like my vision was failing in the most beautiful way. It was like whenever you see a beautiful sunset finishing up and everything just fades away to dusk.

For a while, I'd been calling Angel, as if it could have made any difference. Logic was a long lost friend. I'd been told that if you walked for long enough in the desert, you'd eventually reach an oasis. But I hadn't come across one of those – just the imaginary kind. Why is it that whenever you're looking for something ultra specific, it's the only thing you fail to find? I'd come across all sorts of creatures on my journey – things I would have photographed, had I had a working camera. My mind took photographs of them instead, but mostly my fear captured them in stills. They were predators watching me – a lone, vulnerable, walking piece of flesh. Rattlesnakes, gila monsters, Mexican wolves – the sights I wanted to see from a tour bus, right before my eyes. I tried to avoid eye contact with them and just moved as silently as I could, trying to pretend they were as innocuous as puppies and kittens.

Closing my eyes made no difference. Fear was the only thing lurking in that dark cavity located behind physical vision. I stopped and sat on a rock. There was so much danger around me, but my primary thought was that I couldn't move my mouth anymore. It tasted like dry sand – my lips refused to part. I couldn't taste any moisture for the first time in my life. Maybe, I thought, this was what dying of thirst tasted like.

And then, as I made peace with my demise, I heard the sound of an engine, the screech and halt of tyres. A car door opened – it was as loud as a plane crashing in a fireball, and as unexpected. Standing in front of me was Angel, calling my name.

"Can we put this silly fight behind us, Rob?" she asked, lightly, like we were dealing with something frivolous that we could laugh off tomorrow.

She stood before me, like an open doorway, welcoming me back into the world. Water, warm words and life were right in front of me.

Or was it just a mirage?

## *Moods of the Moon*

Start your story during a full moon night.

1800+ Creative Writing Prompts To Inspire You Right Now (reedsy.com)

The moon is even moodier than me – and I'm a moody person. I always have been, like it or not. Our natural nightlight waxes and wanes and sometimes, I forget that it's even there, but it's always changing. I notice it most when it's round and full, like a ball of white fury suspended in the sky. Strange things happen on a full moon – as legend tells us, but I'd never witnessed any of it until that curious night. I was outside, in the middle of a forest, camping for the first time. It's something I avoided until the age of thirty-five – not by active avoidance – but it was still something I'd never tried.

I was at a makeshift campsite. None of us really knew what we were doing, and our outdoor survival skills were questionable, to put it kindly. We pitched a tent, unsure of whether it would hold up for the evening, and we lit a campfire, hoping it wouldn't spread beyond our small firepit. When things like that go well, I think it comes down to luck more than skill. I've always been more of a bookish type than an outdoor adventurer, but that night awoke a longing for the forest that has never left me.

We were sitting around a campfire, warming our bodies and the milk for our hot chocolate. The crackle of crisping marshmallows was loud in the soundless wood. A few rustles made themselves heard, but the wildlife was shy that evening.

We hadn't seen anything living – to my relief. But the things that come out after dark don't always have to be living to find motion. I felt something glazing my fingertips, like the light touch of a loved one – gentle but undeniable. I retracted my hand from the fireside and scanning it for bugs. There wasn't anything there, but then the dancer took my hand. She twirled around the fire pit, pulling me into her ritualistic dance. I didn't know what it signified, but I wasn't asked about that – I was just initiated into the practice. Whenever I looked at my companions, they were all still seated and none of them appeared to notice my movements. The figures that moved me were flimsy despite their defined movements. Their spirits felt stronger than their bodies – like ethereal angels pulling me into an unwanted waltz. It wasn't a dance I felt comfortable doing. I'm not opposed to a dance in the right conditions – but I need a catchy song and a dark club – somewhere I wouldn't be recognised in daylight. In that strange patch of forest, I felt at my most visible in the darkest of spaces.

I didn't know why we were doing it, but my body was compelled to follow. I'd heard of strange stories being written in dark forests – many of them impromptu scripts composed aloud for the entertainment of friends. I liked feeling spooked by stories. I'd always liked the thrill of a horror story, or of the most unexpected of surprises. But there was something different about being an active participant in a ghostly story. I could hear the music growing in volume, but it had to be my imagination. None of us had a device with us, and the songs weren't something I could have imagined hearing from anyone's playlist. It was old and crackled like an undusted record. The tune was mournful and melancholy. The dances were too, when I thought about them. They weren't energetic or animalistic; they were fluid and forlorn.

I could hear the dancers weeping, but no one else in our campsite seemed stirred by it. It was something only I could hear. I couldn't explain any of it away with logic. Those are the types of stories that scare me the most. I listened to the gentle weeps of the ghosts. Those were the only things I could compare them to – with their translucent skin and their faded appearances. They chanted together and began to sing a song of their own. It was the saddest thing I had ever heard. They sang to the moon like they were begging it for their lives back – whispered messages between themselves and the wind. I've always been an empath – sensitive to the feelings of others – but this was something else entirely – it was something from the spiritual realm.

And then I heard their pleas – they wanted us to move from their home. They were stuck there in the afterlife – a limbo of their own making. We were trespassing on their sacred space. I found my human voice again and told everyone to leave, or something bad was going to happen – like it had happened to those women – their spirits were dancing and singing on, centuries later, trying to relieve themselves of what had happened – a suicide squad on that shared soil.

They'd banded together to comfort each other, having each lost a child, but they had only unearthed the tangled roots of their own grief. They'd spent so much time together in that one spot. The energy was palpable – at least to me. My companions still laughed over the campfire, cracking empty jokes that felt irreverent. I was in a hurry to get us out of there, but I was just the loon of the group – the dancer that swayed with the spirits. I packed up my belongings, rapidly – dumping a bucket of water to dampen the flames of our fire.

Everyone looked at me with deep suspicion – friends I'd had for years that I had never really opened up to – not like those poor women had to each other. I was desperate to leave their land untouched – to stop polluting it with our profanity and our waste. I knew I was talking gibberish. How do you explain an occurrence like that to people that have never experienced anything like it? I'd always been an unswayable atheist – and I'd denied spirituality at every turn, but I was enchanted by it then. We left the forest, and I slurred something about having spotted a bear, by way of explanation. We were in the Canadian wilderness – a bear wasn't something too fantastic to consider; much less fantastic than what I had really seen.

When we got back to civilisation – to the artificial city lights, the man-made bridges, the things that rooted us in our concrete quarters – I felt like I'd lost something special. The relief I should have felt was replaced with an insatiable curiosity. I knew then that my thirst for the mysteries of the forest would never be sated. It wasn't somewhere I thought I could return to en masse. I had to see what there was to find there alone. And so, I braved it – but I never saw a single thing I could liken to that night. Then again, I haven't been back on a full moon. When it's ripe and ready, maybe I'll go back and see what it births for me.

# <u>Divergence in an Upsetting World</u>

Write about a character who develops a special ritual to cope

with something.

1800+ Creative Writing Prompts To Inspire You Right Now (reedsy.com)

I don't cope well with change. OCD is my constant companion and I need to keep it happy at all times. It likes plenty of notice and routine, and predictability. I was diagnosed as a child, so it's nothing new to me, but it becomes much more complex in the life of an adult. I had an appointment cancelled this week, and it felt like the world was ending. I'd had it booked for months. I have to schedule my appointments at regular intervals, or I toss and turn on my memory foam mattress, worrying all night long. The hairdresser doesn't get it. She says she can only slot me in when they're "free." I try my best to ensure I get appointments whenever I need them, but this time, everything went to pot.

I got a phone call on Wednesday morning. I never answer unknown numbers, but this one came up under the name of my hairdressing salon. I thought they'd be phoning with an update about something minor, but they said they had to cancel my appointment. There was a leak in the roof of the salon, and they were in the process of mopping the excess water up. I pictured a few drops, but they said it was like the aftermath of a tsunami. I thought that was an enormous exaggeration, but they had to excuse themselves somehow. They don't know how much that kind of thing rattles me. It upsets my entire month. I stare at my haircut in the bathroom mirror. It has spotlights in there, so you can see every split end. I stand, looking myself in the eye and wallowing in despair. I can't go elsewhere either. My condition won't allow it. I have my one hairdresser, and God help me if she decides to have any children because her period of maternity leave would upturn my entire existence, not to mention destroying my hair. The haircut is simple enough – short back and sides, but it must be done with precision, with the same pair of scissors, stationed in the same seat.

I can't even consider going to a different hairdresser. They might do it differently and I won't be able to settle myself. The discomfort of the wrong haircut feels like leeches making a trail up my neck and circling my skull. It's a feeling so horrible it's hard to find a fitting simile. I tried to distract myself that day, from sitting, waiting beside the phone, willing it to ring with my cancelled cancellation.

People always talk about the main life events – births, deaths, marriages, illnesses. For me, the everyday things have the power to be just as catastrophic when they don't follow my carefully composed plan. I sat, brushing my hair with my palm, feeling the texture that comes with extra length. I hate that feeling. It's like bristles growing on a piece of satin.

I couldn't think of a single thing to make myself feel better, but I knew I had to find something big. Any therapist I've been to has suggested "coping mechanisms," and I've just laughed at them, like they're a quack. We never do leave the appointment better friends than we were before it started. I've been told I'm difficult, but they don't know how difficult it is for me to live with myself. What they have to deal with for a mere moment is nothing compared to that.

I started to format a list of all my concerns. I was writing feverishly, and they were pouring out the pen tip onto the waiting page. The hairdressing ones were top of the list. Maybe to anyone else, they'd be a footnote, but to me they're the main body of the text. I wrote and wrote and wrote by the light of a candle. I was alone with the shadows climbing my walls. We were trying to escape our confinement together, but there wasn't much hope for any of us. The flame of the candle wavered, but my pen never did. I was clear about what was bothering me. As soon as I was finished, I tore the piece of paper into tiny pieces, and I torched the fragments on the candle. Then I sprinkled the ash around me, like emptying an urn. The mess of everything was visible in front of me and I felt better. I could still feel the annoyance in the hairs on my head, but it was lessened inside my brain.

I left the ash there. It was still smouldering, which was probably a bit dangerous, but it was a thrill too. I never broke any rules or made a mess of things. Only other people did that. I got a glimpse of what it was like to feel like I was diverging from the fixed route. It felt addictive. I wanted to take it further, but I didn't. I was toying with danger without doing it to a dangerous degree. The room glowed in the low light. The day was ending, and I had made it through in one piece, thanks only to my new-found ritual. I couldn't stop the unwanted actions of others, but I could destroy them in physical form. I went to bed that night with a clear head and feeling of quietude. That's something I never get, so it was remarkable.

The next morning, the sun came up and brought with it an array of new nuisances. It's hard to avoid them in this imperfect world. The hairdresser phoned me to reschedule my missed appointment. It wouldn't be on the exact weekday I wanted, but it was better than worrying about it for another month. That was resolved, but nothing stays resolved for long. An hour later, I found out that my food delivery was missing several items. I started to get into a sad state over it, but then I remembered the new ritual I'd found, and I sat down at the table, ready to burn away some more woes. I might have burnt the house down, but it was worth the risk – saying goodbye to angst over that unfilled shopping list.

# No Such Thing as Ghosts

Write about a character in a situation where they have to be

brave for someone else's sake.

1800+ Creative Writing Prompts To Inspire You Right Now (reedsy.com)

Claude was always chasing ghosts. He'd promised Julia that he'd be back in ten minutes, but more time than that had elapsed, and he was nowhere to be seen. The house was so fragile looking; it almost seemed to sway like a leaf in the breeze, but it was made of brick and mortar. Its lack of upkeep was the problem. It had been standing there since Victorian days, but with no maintenance in decades. Julia still thought it had a beautiful face, but behind the face lurked bad thoughts. It was famous in the neighbourhood for being condemned. Julia had never felt the inclination to enter it. She wasn't drawn to things like that. She didn't even believe in the spiritual world. She liked to see everything in front of her in solid matter before she took it into consideration. But the place still gave her the creeps.

Claude and she met when they were little. They'd always lived in the same town and neither of them had progressed beyond that. They had no goals beyond living and dying there. It was a picturesque place – like somewhere that stars as the perfect site on a postcard. Only the residents knew the back story there. Vic House was somewhere that was talked about regularly and no one had to explain why. It was well known if you came from the area. Julia got chills whenever she passed it, and she'd never known how. It had a feel to it, and she didn't put stock in such things. Those four intricately sculpted walls contained the definition of creepy. Julia thought it was sad that no one had saved them from disrepair, but there was no salvaging a place after an event like that.

The house was filled with misery in its former years. A family had lived there with a tyrant of a father. She'd heard the story countless times: he had killed his own family. People said he was possessed and that the place had always housed destructive energy. There was a certain inevitability to the act.

She hoped Claude would come back in a minute, or she'd be forced to go inside. She could think of hundreds of unappealing things she'd rather do. The street was tranquil. It lulled you into a false sense of security, relaxing your worries until they bled away. But then came the bang. It was more like a demolition than a clatter. The sound reminded Julia of those scheduled demolitions she'd seen on TV – when the building implodes and then, dust. Julia's stomach sank; not in the gradual dipping way it does when you're anxious - in a rollercoaster style drop. She ran to the door, her hand hesitated on the handle and then she burst through in a 3, 2, 1 reveal. She expected carnage before her – or at least a collapsed staircase, but all was still. Claude wasn't there. She wondered where he lingered and why he had taken so long. Had he hurt himself? She wondered if she'd find him somewhere, skewered on metal, like meat awaiting cooking. He wasn't in the hallway, or on the landing. She walked tentatively towards her friend. Now she knew why she'd avoided it all – she was terrified of the ghostly world. There was enough to fear in the material one: the one where she had some sense of control. Here, she didn't know what she was doing. She was like an untaught driver behind the wheel of a careening car.

"Claude," she called out in a loud whisper. "Are you there?" She approached the kitchen door, and she turned its rusty handle, pushing open the mahogany mass. It had the weight of a dead body, and it creaked like nothing in a horror movie ever had. There, she heard the unmatched bang – the one that sounded like floors of a building collapsing, smacking one into the next as they gave in. There was nothing there – just some chipped dishes displayed in a cabinet, a grandfather clock that had stopped ticking long ago and a disused range, so delipidated that no estate sale could have marketed it.

Julia turned back on herself, trying to distance herself from the violence of the noise. She mightn't have seen anything, but she was filled with terror. She could feel herself involuntarily shivering. The place was cold, but it was July, and she knew it wasn't because of the temperature. Her body was responding with shock, and she couldn't dismiss the fear she felt with logic. She was facing her greatest fear – the one she hadn't fully identified with until she'd entered that building – the unreachable realm of ghosts. She didn't know the full extent to which they could hurt humans, but the bounds of the spiritual world were ever-expanding and incomprehensibly limitless.

"Claude," she continued to call, but it didn't come out with volume. If Claude was still in the building, or still in the same spiritual sphere as her, she knew he couldn't hear her. He'd always been a wild, wandering kind of soul, prone to bouts of curiosity that led him into dangerous situations. She'd always accompanied him like a good friend does, but she preferred to stand in the shade, waiting for him to finish up in the direct sunlight.

The rooms of the downstairs of that house of grandeur were all achingly empty. She ascended the staircase, creating a creak with every footstep she took. It would have been laughably horrific, had it not been so terror-inducing. She felt it in every fibre of her being – the distilled fear that stood up inside her: a kind of fright she'd never known she was capable of feeling. There were so many doors in the place that it was hard to know where to begin. They were all firmly closed, which made it much more difficult. Her own two hands were the pair that had to do the opening: the opening onto a world of impenetrable possibility.

She took possession of the first door handle, held it with long consideration and then opened it. She was quaking with fear of she knew not what. That was what made it so palpably chilling. "Claude," she called, feebly. "Are you in here?" Her eyes met the multitude of mirrors facing her, like a moment of horror in a Hitchcock movie. She was met with her own reflection – fear mirrored around her on every surface. She turned away from it and then the door slammed closed. Claude was standing behind it, smiling – if you could call it that. It was more of a leer.

"Boo," he boomed.

She jumped. It was sudden and she didn't like the strange look in his eyes.

She couldn't form a word.

He could. He was in his favourite place.

"I thought you said you didn't believe in ghosts."

She shuddered. She'd faced her fear for his sake, but she knew they needed to get out of there quickly, to escape that building's influence.

# Cutting the Comedy

Set your story on a film or TV set, starting with someone

calling "Cut!"

"Cut!"

Everyone snapped out of what they'd been doing. They were like dreamers beckoned back to disappointing reality. They all looked at the one stern face. The room was unfathomably expansive. Everyone watching the filmed version sees the set, but they don't see the surroundings that seem to go on for miles, with hundreds of people, cameras, microphones on poles. It's like stepping back from the world and seeing the rest of the universe. You realise that the set only contains a small section of a story, and it often has a different atmosphere to the real stage.

Gil was hollering as usual. He said that Sophie had messed up her line. It was wrongly phrased. She'd swapped a couple of the words around, so the line lost its punch. That was what he said anyway – no one else had noticed.

"I wanted to go to that park today," had become "Today, I wanted to go to the park."

The next remarkable incident wasn't announced for another line: she lost her pants to the neighbour's dog. That was the main event in the script; not an unremarkable sentence stating the location of the upcoming scene, but Gil was a control freak. He sat in his folding chair that seemed to buckle under his weight. He lived on cheeseburgers that he got hand-delivered to his chair at regular intervals throughout his working day. The hands that offered them up were often shaking. He wore a baseball cap that hid his face until he decided to show it. He had a way of looking you dead in the eyeballs whenever he wanted to.

Sophie was ready for the onslaught that came after a small mistake. She was trembling, but she hoped her physical distance from Gil's chair meant that he couldn't completely see it. That was his favourite thing to witness though – a person that had arrived with confidence, reduced to a wispy, wavering leaf – something that could be torn by the slightest change in the air.

She looked around at her fellow actors, hoping someone brave would step in, but Gil had a habit of reducing the most brazen character to a cowering child in the corner.

"Do it right this time, or you lose the rest of your day," he barked.

The rest of the film crew followed suit. It was like they'd all taken some sort of potion that brought them under his strange spell. No one dared counter him.

The scene should have been relatively straightforward: dog runs in, woman loses her pants, dog transforms them into a chew toy, everyone laughs on cue. There weren't a million different camera angles – it was just a straight scene. The actors' delivery was the only factor that mattered. Maybe that was why Gil was being especially harsh. He'd already made them redo it forty times in a row. Sophie could feel her mouth drying out from overuse and underwatering. She'd left her water bottle on the far side of the room, planning to retrieve it after the quick scene had been captured (which she thought would have been done and dusted two hours ago.) She thought about running over to get it, but she was too afraid to attempt it. She knew the smallest disobedience might set Gil off, and she didn't feel like listening to a day-long, one-sided shouting match.

Curtis gave her a small smile. It would have been imperceptible to anyone on the crew. He knew what she'd been through. He'd had his fair share of criticism too.

The pressure in the room was mounting. Everyone looked like they were sweating enough to create a sprinkler system. Gil looked cool and composed, but bullies always do. They like to see everyone else writhing under their gaze, but they never look the least bit disturbed by it. In fact, they live for it. His chair audibly creaked as he leaned forwards to micromanage the scene. He removed his sunglasses, which he always wore indoors. He said they shaded his eyes from the startling light of the spotlights, but Sophie thought they were just an accessory worn for effect. He pushed the sunglasses on top of his hair. It held his greasy, overgrown strands from his face, but it didn't make him look any more appealing. He was just had a presence – one of those indefinable ones that fills up an entire room. The fear he produced in others filled the room – growing into every crevice like vines in a fairy tale, and just as destructive.

"From the top," he said, standing up from his chair, spitting burger gristle onto the pristine floor.

"Action," said the guy with the clapperboard. He slammed it shut in a way that looked undecided and sloppy. Gil shot him a look of warning.

The film was supposed to be light-hearted – a chick flick that cheered up roomfuls of comedy seekers. The actors hoped that would come across. It felt like it would take a miracle for it to extract a laugh from a single viewer. There certainly hadn't been a single one on set since they'd started filming.

Curtis was the perfect co-star to have. He had a calming presence, even though he was just as scared as everyone else. Sophie swore that she'd walk away from Gil on the last day of filming, waving her flag of freedom. She almost wanted the film to be a flop, just to spite him. He deserved some disappointment after his months-long tyranny, his self-awarded ruling over all cast members and crew. They were people too, whether they were viewed as such or not. They would return to their own lives at the end of the long day, with volition. If they were lucky, their home lives would show up the inhumanity of the film world.

Sophie's dreams of what Hollywood could have been ran through her mind as she overthought every one of her gestures, her facial expressions and her vocal tone. She knew she'd never get it quite right. The practice round of lines shared by the actors around the table was the best they'd perform, and no one would else ever see it. It had felt like a special kind of magic there, but here, in front of Gil, they had lost it. He had a way of shattering the magic for everyone. His favourite burger delivery guy didn't even get a tip. The servitude shown by all the people in that hall was something he had dreamed of since he was a small, round boy in school, named after a famous pig. He could still hear the taunting when he closed his eyes at night and silence found him. When he was in his folding chair, that felt like an uncomfortable deckchair and that didn't adequately support his generous posterior and that was beneath what he deserved, he could finally stand up to them all. In his little world of film, he could repay his enemies of childhood for stealing something important from him: the right to be joyful and free.

Sophie hoped at the end of filming she'd still remember what that feeling felt like. Curtis hoped Sophie would be OK. Maybe whenever it was all over, they'd go for a drink together – they'd have an unbreakable connection that only a trauma bond can create. In the end, Gil would lose, and they would win. While shooting lasted, Gil could enjoy the false glory in the kingdom he'd created, and maybe they'd even manage to make someone laugh, just to spite him.

# *On Pink Earth*

Set your story in a rosy-pink world where everything is

rainbows and unicorns... until it isn't.

**1800+ Creative Writing Prompts To Inspire You Right Now**

**(reedsy.com)**

Perfect, perfect, perfect; that's how every day of our lives is. In this world of pink, I am a humble member of the cast. I have the luck to wake up to it every morning. Everything appears in different hues of pink. That's my favourite colour. It's everyone's favourite colour here. When the pink is pure, we know that all is well in our world. It's like a barometer of what's going on. Pink is perfection.

I get up every day and step out of my veiled bed. I walk across the plush carpet that feels like velvet beneath my feet. My nails are perfectly manicured, and I have a dressing table with everything laid out in a perfect kind of parallel symmetry. I go through my morning routine. It never becomes monotonous. I take my time over everything and there is nothing to worry about. Life is a holiday. I just make myself up, style my hair and get ready for the great day ahead. Breakfast awaits me on the table. No one has a servant because no one needs to work. Everything we need falls in front of us, as if by magic. When I arrive at the breakfast table, there is a stack of waffles or pancakes awaiting me. Freshly brewed coffee fills my favourite cup. It has steam that rises and forms a heart shape in the air, directly above the centre of the cup. I drink it at the speed I choose. I'm alone but that doesn't matter. We are all alone in our little bubbles. When we step outside our front door, that's when we interact with the rest of the people in our world. I have a dog called Sippy. He likes to accompany me on walks. He isn't much work to look after. The machinations of our world take care of everyone and everything. He satisfies my need for companionship. It just works better being apart from others. We have visitors whenever we want – lovely little parties where we are all delighted to see each other.

I walk down the street with a bounce in my step, my ponytail dancing in the light breeze. The sunshine is predictably glorious, and there is only ever a soft breeze, so it never gets too hot. The park is filled with smiling citizens, and I am one with them. We are all in this together and there is a feeling of camaraderie that I couldn't imagine existing in another world. I take Sippy for a walk around the park, and we greet everyone we pass. We all know each other on a first name basis, and we call each other friends. There aren't too many of us, so nowhere is ever overcrowded. Waiting isn't something we are ever forced to do. The trees are all the same shade of pink with bark that is smooth and lacks texture. No one could get a splinter if they tried to; in fact, injuries don't exist here – nothing unseemly does. I've never even had a crease in my clothing, and I never have to iron – unless I want to, of course. We only do the things that we feel the desire to do. There are special surprises around every corner. Predictability gets boring when there's too much of it, so there is always plenty of novelty here.

A beautiful bunch of flowers awaited me whenever I got back to my house that day. There was a card attached to them. An admirer had sent them. I couldn't think of a possible admirer of mine. I only knew people on a friendly basis, so I was truly perplexed by the flowers' arrival. The bouquet was an exotic mix. They weren't pink, which was strange. They stood out in stark contrast against the pink backdrop. My eyes weren't used to the sight of them, and the brightness almost stung them and activated my tear ducts. They were exciting in a way I'd never experienced before. I put them into a pink vase filled with pink water and they looked like they weren't really at home there. They didn't match anything in the house, but they intrigued me.

I'd been told tales of items that weren't pink, of how they could enter from the outside world. I'd been warned not to get too close to them. There was poison behind the colourful exterior – or so they said. I didn't know anyone personally that had seen anything that didn't follow the rules of pink perfection, so there was no way to know for sure. I just knew that the multicoloured flowers had an allure I couldn't deny. I wanted to know the source of them. It was just natural human curiosity. When things are perfect, we aren't supposed to question them. It would be like being in the garden of Eden and tasting forbidden apples. I don't put a lot of stock in cautionary tales though; especially whenever you can't find a real example to back them up.

I touched the petals of the flowers and looked dreamily out the window at the beautiful scene outside. A pink waterfall ran over smooth baby pink rocks and pooled in a lake that was so still even the water's movement didn't disturb it. I'd been looking at all the shades of pink for a lifetime and I had never tired of it. I had no reason to look beyond it. I'd been told that we had the perfect world. No one outside it lived like we did. There were shades of colour that I was lucky not to have seen, or so I was told. It was hard to believe what anyone said when they acted informed but they hadn't seen it for themselves.

I was satisfied with the way everything was, but I couldn't completely silence my curiosity either. It ate away at me at night, when everything was still and I was lying with my head in the perfect dip of my pink pillows, fluffed up like two marshmallows.

I didn't toss and turn for too long. That doesn't happen in our world. Discomfort doesn't exist, so it can't, even whenever you have a head full of questions.

Morning came and I went through my breakfast routine. That day, I had a stack of fresh pancakes, strawberries, whipped cream and chocolate chips, and I would never gain a pound from it. I devoured it with relish and drank my coffee, looking at the straightness of the pictures on the walls. Nothing ever sat askew. I got myself up whenever I'd taken my repose and the dishes vanished from the table. There wasn't a crumb to clean up; everything had always been that neat, but I never took it for granted for a second, because appreciation is also important in our perfect world.

I went for my morning shower, took my selected outfit from the rotating wardrobe and touched my cheeks to bring make-up to my face. I felt energised, like I did every single day. I couldn't wait to see what lay ahead. Before I had time to run through my planner and see what fun activities awaited me, I heard a strange sound. I'd never heard the doorbell ring before – not unless I was expecting guests and it was their arrival time, (right on the dot.) I walked downstairs, unsure of how to approach the situation. It was a complete unknown.

Whenever I got closer to the door, I could see a tall figure's silhouette behind the glass. Whenever I pulled the door ajar, there was a man standing in front of me. He was striking because he was dressed from head to foot in a colour I'd never seen before. It looked like it was all one shade, but I just knew it wasn't pink. He winked at me and smiled. I opened the door wider, considering inviting him in. He looked pleasant, even though his clothing was foreign to me. I knew he wasn't from our world, but I was curious about him.

"I sent you some flowers," he said. "I was going to remain anonymous, but I wanted to talk to you."

I could feel myself blushing, but I doubted it changed my complexion. I was as pink as could be, in different tones, but as pink as anything else around me. His face was a different hue, and his lips weren't pink, but I didn't know what to call the colour of them.

"Would you like to come in?" I asked. It felt like I was breaking every rule I'd ever been taught, but he seemed harmless too.

"How did you find me?" I asked, leaning towards him.

I thought of how lovely it would be to have afternoon tea to offer him and it was immediately before us – tiered cake-stand, and everything. He didn't look surprised by it. He just took a cup and a plate like it was all completely natural to him. He winked at me again. I didn't know where to begin to talk to him. I had no idea who he was and what he wanted from me; but I suddenly wanted to ask him a million questions.

"I saw you from afar," he said. "I came here by mistake, but I couldn't leave again. I had to get your attention, but then, I was worried you would avoid me because of everything you've been told.

"Where are you from?" I asked him.

"I'm from outside your world. You don't want to know about mine."

"Why not?"

"I'm sure you'd like to know what exists there, but once you know, you can't regain your naivety."

I looked at him confusedly. I had no idea what that meant. No one had ever said that word to me before.

"I really do want to know," I said.

"The more I tell you, the more it affects your world."

"What do you mean?"

"I can't explain it to you – it's just better if you stay with what you know now."

"Tell me one thing about it," I said, nearly spilling my tea in anticipation of what he'd tell me. I'd never done that before. Spillages weren't something I'd ever seen occur. I didn't make a mess, but he nodded at my hand.

"See," he said, "Even my presence changes things."

"Then why did you come here?"

"Because I was transfixed."

"Transfixed by what?"

"Your strange beauty."

"Why is it strange?"

"I've never seen anything like it before."

"But you have been in our world for a while?"

"Just for a few days."

"You must have seen others like me."

"No, it has nothing to do with the pinkness. It transcends that. I'll tell you about how I got here."

I looked at him. He was spellbinding. I'd never seen anything like his looks before. His facial expressions were completely different too. He had furrows in his brow and his lips fell whenever he looked serious. He didn't look perpetually pleasant.

"I was playing around with some voodoo stuff at a friend's house. It was a game that sends you to different realms, but we thought it was just a laugh. We were playing it together and my friend got creeped out and left the room. I decided to keep going. As it turns out, curiosity does kill the cat."

I didn't know what he was talking about. It made perfect sense linguistically, but there were so many concepts I didn't understand. I'd never heard of someone being "creeped out" or of curiosity killing pets.

I crossed over here, and I thought I was dreaming at first – one of those lucid dreams where you can't differentiate between being awake and asleep, but now I know that game somehow brought me here.

"Will you leave again?"

"I don't know how to, but I don't want to now either. It's a beautiful place. Lacking in colour – but it's lacking a lot of other bad things we have too.

"What like?"

"Crime, unkindness, poverty."

"I don't know what those are."

"That's what's so beautiful – that naivety."

I shook my head at him – letting him know I didn't understand again, but he didn't seem to mind, and he smiled at me. His smile was warm, but it lacked something the other smiles I'd seen in my life had. There was something hanging behind it that I couldn't express in words.

"What's your name?" he asked me.

"It's Serenity."

"Of course it is," he smiled.

"I'm Chris... Can I stay here with you?"

"I don't see why not," I said. "It's just me and my dog, Sippy. I haven't lived with anyone since I moved out of my family home."

"Not with anyone?"

"No, we don't live with anyone – unless we decide to get married."

"I wonder why. Does no one ever break up?"

"Do you mean leave each other? No, I've never heard of it. Everyone that gets married is happy together. They're happy when they're on their own too. They're happy in general."

"That's what's so interesting about here."

"I want to know about what else there is outside."

"Trust me, you don't," he said.

He offered to sleep on the sofa. I didn't know sofas were for sleeping on, but he didn't seem to mind. There mustn't have been real comfort where he came from. I didn't know what his world was like, but I knew there was a huge amount of information I didn't know. I went to sleep, but I had a bad dream. I woke up with a feeling I'd never had before. I saw colours I had never seen before. My body was violently shaking.

When I got out of bed and went to complete my usual routine, Chris was there. The breakfast table was messy but there was still food on it. It just wasn't how it usually looked. I took a waffle and offered some more to Chris. He had finished eating and he waved his hand at me, like he was telling me he was busy. He was rolling something I hadn't seen before. He put some straggly bits into a piece of paper and rolled it up. Then he lit it. It smelled strongly and it made me cough. He exhaled and I asked what he was doing.

"Smoking – I'm addicted, sadly."

"Is it a bad thing?"

"It can kill you."

"Why does anyone do it?"

"Stress, probably – and other reasons."

"I don't know what stress is."

"Aren't you lucky?" he said with a smile that didn't look completely well-wishing.

As I looked at him, I noticed that something strange was happening to my eyesight. The pristine pink furniture looked like it was covered in dark blotches. I rubbed my eyes, but whenever I removed my hands, it had spread even more. The pink was changing to a different tone. It didn't look perfect anymore. I saw my reflection in the mirror. I didn't either; I had stains on my skin. Chris didn't say anything. He didn't appear to see it. I didn't feel good, but I didn't know why. There was a new feeling spreading all over my body and I wanted to lie down.

A sharp sound came at the door. The wood of it cracked; the glass window shattering into tiny shards. I jumped. Some people barged through the door wielding a weapon. They were wearing a lot of heavy armour. I couldn't see their faces. They were still dressed from head to toe in pink. They seized Chris by the arm and pulled him onto his feet, twisting his arm behind his back. They put some metal rings on his wrists and snapped them shut.

"What's happening?" I managed to whisper. I got a feeling I'd never experienced before. It felt like my stomach was suddenly sitting in my throat.

"They found the portal – thanks to him," someone said. "Everything has been contaminated."

I didn't know who "they" were, but I just saw a look of disappointment spreading over Chris' face. The room was changing colour. The pink was all but gone. The colours looked ugly to me. They didn't resemble the exotic flowers he'd given me one bit.

"I guess we won't get our happily ever after, after all," said Chris.

Then, they roughly led him out the door.

I stood in the dim toned room, feeling strange to be alone. For the first time in my life, I didn't know what on Pink Earth to do with myself.

# *Childhoods of Confinement*

Set your entire story in a car.

1800+ Creative Writing Prompts To Inspire You Right Now (reedsy.com)

"We're locked in," said Karen, sullenly.

"What's new?" asked Phil, picking at the bobbles on the fabric of the seat. It'd had a speckled texture to it when it was new, but it hadn't aged well.

"Something exciting might happen, you never know."

"Does anything exciting ever happen?"

Karen peered out the window. There was no one around them, except a few vacant cars with no other passengers locked in the back seats. Driving to the pub wasn't unusual then, neither was driving home.

"What do they do in there for so long?" Karen asked.

"Drink themselves silly and talk about everything we aren't allowed to hear."

Karen picked up her battered comic. She'd been reading the same one for several months and the print was starting to fade in places, but she knew it off by heart anyway. Her comics were her best friends. Despite the fact that she and her brother were stuck in the same confinement, they were enemies more often than they were friends.

She felt her tummy rumble and wondered what time dinner would be on the table at that day. They'd been promised a trip to the beach that weekend, but Dad had had a rough week in work, so here they were, at his usual resting place.

They'd come to loathe the look of The Winfield pub. It was in one of those old red brick buildings with a wooden sign – one that had never been changed and the letters were fading away. It didn't need to be labelled; the regulars knew where they were going, drunk or sober. There wasn't much happening in that area: no kids, no life, just a lone pub. Now and again, they'd see an old drunk stumble out of it and make their weary way down the road. Their minds would make up stories about the person, like minds tend to do in their deepest state of boredom. Unremarkable people suddenly became interesting characters in their mind's creations.

Philip held onto his tin car. He drove it over his knee and up the back of the empty driver's seat. He drove it across the window, weaving around the waterdrops that fell every day in Belfast; at least, it felt like they did. It was a suitable accompaniment to the mood of their lives. Everything was grey, dreary and uninspiring. It felt like they would never escape their imprisonment in that cell of a car. If it wasn't the car, it was their bedroom. Most of the time, they just went back and forth between the two places. The most excitement they got was whenever the neighbourhood kids got together in the street and made a rope swing on the lamppost. That kept them busy for hours. They were very civilised about it, taking it in turns and waiting patiently. Time was meaningless in days as lengthy as that and none of them were spoilt. Nobody could afford to spoil their kids – at least not anybody that they knew personally.

Karen traced her finger around the raindrops on the window, making pictures with her imagination. She chased a few with her index finger as they slid down the glass, meeting them at the end of their path.

"What time do you think they'll come out at today?"

"What's the point in asking me that? If you count every second, it'll feel like forever."

He was getting irritable with her. She could sense it like hounds hear change in the air. He reminded her of her dad when he got like that: short-tempered and snappy. Everyone deals with stress differently. Karen buried her head in her magazine again, getting lost in the safe worlds of her favourite cartoons. She often wished she could climb inside the pages and stay tucked in there, becoming part of a better story. The kids in her comics had a voice. They got to be cheeky to adults and push the boundaries. She'd never dared do that. Even when she was faultlessly polite and respectful, she still always ended up in trouble.

It was the era of "children should be seen and not heard," and making any sort of fuss only attracted unpleasant attention. She willed her parents to come back, but simultaneously, treasured the peace while it lasted. Either way, she felt unbalanced, like something dangerous could happen at any moment.

The pub door opened. It stayed open for a minute without exposing the person behind it. They sat, feeling anxious and hopeful, mixed together in one big ball they carried in their little stomachs. That ball was always there, and they never got a chance to forget it, unless they got lost in a child's game to the point that they forgot reality. Karen and Philip had more in common than they knew how to express. They were too young and emotionally ill-equipped to express it, to learn that the other one was having the same waves of emotion at the same time. They weren't alone, but they couldn't have felt more alone, sitting side by side. Being unable to communicate with a sibling isn't much different to being an only child.

After their long moment of anticipation, a man appeared through the door. They knew him by face but not by name. He must have frequented the pub as much as their parents did. There were only ever locals at that time. Everyone stayed in their own pockets of Belfast, safe with what they knew. The Troubles were in full force, and everything was always tumultuous. You weren't even safe in your home, never mind in the other side's business or in their area. That added a thread of tension to everything. Even whenever things were settled at home, they were still anxious about the next thing that would kick off. Inside their small terrace, or outside in their carefully contained world – it was all equally stifling and terrifying.

For five minutes, there was silence in the car and silence outside. Not a person passed. Not a single sound came from the roads. And then the blast came – the unfathomable blast that blew out the pub front. They couldn't make sense of it. The shock kept them strapped in their seats, even without seatbelts. No one bothered with them then. Their parents were inside that building. Bad people or good, their guides in life were right at the heart of the blast.

# <u>A Story of Space, Left</u>

Set your story after aliens have officially arrived on Earth.

1800+ Creative Writing Prompts To Inspire You Right Now (reedsy.com)

"They're not how I thought they'd look at all," said Rachel, reflectively. "You just assume they'll look like all the pictures we've seen."

"If you went to Biblical times and saw Jesus, you'd probably think the same thing. People make guesses at things, but they're usually wrong."

"It's hard to be accurate about something you've never seen."

"True," said Kerry, sighing. "We were lucky not to know anything then - they're coming in droves now."

"Yeah, it might take a while, but I think they'll eventually completely take over."

"What was wrong with their home planet?"

"I guess they're like us. They can't leave anything alone and just been satisfied with what they have."

Kerry gazed out the window and thought about all the shut down possibilities of the ever-expansive world they'd once had. Since their arrival, everything had taken on a different tone.

Florida looked changed now, even whenever the aliens weren't visible. You never knew when you'd run into the next one. She would always remember with glassy clarity the day they first arrived. They'd come in something that was less flying saucer and more space bubble. It looked like it could have been popped with a pin prick. If only. They'd survived and traversed the galaxy in it, and they'd made good time too. They couldn't communicate the details, but their return trips showed just how quickly they could go there and come back. They hadn't brought any physical items with them, but they took up a lot of space.

The streets were mostly bare, the beaches emptied. Kerry had always been used to the coming and goings from the neighbouring beach at Clearwater. People had stopped swimming and they'd stopped sunbathing. She didn't know why everyone had; maybe it was just because word spreads and people unthinkingly copy each other whenever they're scared. Kerry had thought she was brave until the aliens' arrival. It's hard to be brave when faced with the unknown and they had looked much different to a friendly ET. They were larger than humans and grotesque to their eyes. They didn't have smiling faces. They didn't really have faces – just holes for seeing and feeding. They were charcoal grey in colour, with long, spidery limbs. The first person that had spotted them had allegedly dropped dead, dying of heart failure from the sheer shock of the vision before them. They'd found her soulless body, but it had taken a while to attribute it to that. They mightn't ever have connected the two events had they not had recurrent encounters in that very area.

Sometimes Kerry wondered why they hit that area first - of all the places on the globe. Was it just a coincidence or did they intentionally select it? It was a place of beauty, but Kerry wondered if it was the most appealing place from bird's eye view? Maybe they had heard reports of life on Earth before they'd even come in to land. They were a form of intelligent life – more intelligent than humans everywhere – even though humans thought themselves the cleverest of species. If they were, they could have done more to fend them off. It felt like the human population was dwindling and there was no single event they could pin it on. The aliens were taking over in a slow, insidious way. The buildings were being razed to the ground. Kerry hated looking at the rubble. It was unclear what was being put there as replacement for them. The aliens didn't share their plans. Even if they'd had blueprints, they couldn't have translated them for human understanding. There was a feeling of finality on Earth – a slow surrender that was spreading across the surface of the world. Broadcasting had broken down. The internet was no longer used. Screens were obsolete. There was no way of communicating between different countries anymore. At first, yes, but then they did away with it all, bit by bit. Kerry kept waiting for something bad to come to her, personally; she just didn't know exactly when or what it would be.

She kept her door triple bolted every night – something she had never felt the need to do before 2035. The place she'd lived in was so poster perfect that it felt like nothing untoward could ever have happened there. That's what made it more shocking and out of the ordinary. Kerry reflected on the pandemic of 2020. It seemed like a mere blip compared with the Alien Invasion. A decade earlier, people still disputed the existence of extra-terrestrial life. It seemed laughable now – the earthly worries they'd had. There had been nothing of that magnitude then; Purely People Problems: that was what they were referred to now and often scoffed at, labelled trivial concerns.

Every night whenever Kerry went to sleep, she considered the fact it might be her last night on Earth. So many people had disappeared, and no one could say what had happened to them, which made it so much worse. Kerry thought of a few of her closest friends, tearfully. She tried not to dwell on their disappearances too much, because it achieved nothing, and survival had to be her priority. If she could evade the aliens, they couldn't do what they'd done to the others. But each week, whenever she saw the empty streets, she wondered if it might be better to join the others, wherever they were. She didn't want to be the last one remaining. That would be petrifying in a way that gathered up every feeling of terror she'd ever experienced and played them out in a single moment. At least Rachel was there too. She wasn't entirely alone, yet. Her family might have vanished one by one, she might have lost all sense of community, and she might have lost every place she'd ever known to the invaders. But she still had Rachel, and each day they met up without anything eventful to tell was a small success.

For weeks, months and years, they escaped it together. Luck was the only thing that could explain it. It was fitting that they were together whenever they finally had their personal encounter with the aliens. They were toasting each other over a quiet dinner, eating some hearty mac and cheese and cornbread when the tendrils appeared around the doorway, coming to beckon them to their shared fate. They were whisked away, so quickly they couldn't gasp; the evidence they'd lived and dined there removed - apart from a few cornbread crumbs.

# Greta's Greatest Gift

Write a story starring an octogenarian who's more than meets

the eye.

**1800+ Creative Writing Prompts To Inspire You Right Now**

**(reedsy.com)**

Nothing stood out about Greta. She lived in a little cottage
with a welcoming glow in the windows. She seemed to lead a
quiet existence. She kept her house tidy and did all her own
chores. She was vivacious for an eighty-year-old, but not to
the point in raised any eyebrows. She kept up the habit her
mother had taught her, of baking a loaf of bread each day.
She'd grown up in the Great Depression and she knew how to
squeeze the best value out of a dollar. Her kitchen was simple,
but it was always sparklingly clean. The aroma of bread
browning in the oven filled the whole household. She had
plenty of friends that dropped in for tea. She served them jam
on bread and hot, milky tea. They never wanted to leave
again; they were so taken in by her charming home and the
warmth of her presence. It felt like a hug to an affection-
starved soul.

Most of Greta's friends were friends she had had for decades.
They had grown up in that very town. People didn't tend to
move around as much then, unless they had an unavoidable
reason to do so. She'd known them in every stage of life, and
they had inseverable bonds; but one of Greta's friends was
new. She had only known Marsha for a year or two. She was
notably younger than her and she inspired interest from the
surrounding community, because no one could quite figure

out why she was there. However, they knew just how predictably kind Greta was. They supposed she must have been a niece of hers or a more distant family member that didn't bear any resemblance to Greta.

Marsha tended to arrive after dark more often than in daylight. She didn't cause as much of a stir in the close-knit community whenever she did that. She could sneak into the cottage and talk to Greta in peace, shielded by the heavy, plush curtains. They talked all night, and Marsha often wondered when Greta slept and why she could do without it at her age. She had more energy than all the kids in the neighbourhood combined.

Marsha pulled an envelope from her bag. She opened it in a way that made Greta brighten with excitement. Their next assignment had arrived. Greta loved the firm. She'd built it out of her own imagination, and it performed well. She didn't tell people she knew that she was a private investigator. She didn't want the neighbours to know what she was up to. She knew all too well how nosy people could be and that was the kind of late-life career choice that would prompt questions. Greta was brought up to believe that you shouldn't ask someone questions unless the person chose to bring the subject up first, but she noticed that many others hadn't received that instruction. By the dim light of the fire, she opened the envelope and began to read. Her eyes were sharp for her age. She didn't like having to play the part of the ailing pensioner. She was anything but vulnerable. She could have run circles around most of the police force, but being an elderly bread-baking neighbourly type that pruned plants and performed small acts of kindness allowed her to live two lives, and that suited her. She kept her privacy and people assumed that she was just a regular grandmother.

She skim-read the letter. It was from a lady that suspected her abducted sister was murdered by a family member, but the case had gone cold a long time ago. Greta sank back into her luxuriously soft cushions. She loved the supple seat on which she had got to the bottom of so many crimes and injustices. She spotted the details others missed; even skilled professionals that had badges and thought they had more brains than she did. She knew when to be quiet and when to observe. That was the secret of her success.

Marsha got up and added another log to the smouldering fire. She prodded it with the poker, and it flared up, roaring with satisfaction. Marsha felt the shivers leave her skin. She'd walked there on foot – for a mile in the depths of Winter. Once she got inside Greta's cottage, she never wanted to leave again. It was deliciously homely, and she felt like she was spending time with her own cherished but departed grandmother. She'd had eyes like an eagle too and she spent a lot of time in quiet observation, but she could cut through a conversation with a single sentence. She was as sharp as a serrated knife. Marsha smiled at Greta as she watched her studying the letter. She read and reread it with a precision that people didn't tend to approach tasks with anymore. Marsha worked in a secretarial role that bored her on a daily basis, so she'd sought out something exciting on the side. Little did she know she'd end up being the sidekick to an eighty-year old private investigator – and one that had solved plenty of cases abandoned by the police.

"We have to take this one on," exclaimed Greta. "I can't wait to sink my teeth into it."

"Even though you have dentures?" Marsha teased.

"My dentures are sharper than most people's original set," she said, laughing to herself.

That sense of humour was what made working with her such a delight. She had the ability to switch from serious investigator to humorous friend to kind, old bread-baking grandmother, and she never got tired. Marsha hoped she'd be as vivacious at that stage of life.

The woman that had disappeared was only twenty years old and she was presumed missing by choice. The police had labelled her a runaway and given up on finding her years before. Greta turned the photo of the woman over in her hand, looking for writing on the back. No one really did that anymore, but someone had scrawled her name with a heart beside it. The heart had a jagged crack down the middle, and it was dated before the date of death. She was smiling in the photo; she had no idea what was coming to her then. Greta had always loved a good detective novel; the kind of thing you could dive into without budging an inch from your toasty armchair. Getting to solve real-life cases was her life's dream and at the age of eighty, she realised, it was never too late to become someone else. She'd find the truth about the woman in the photo, and she thought she'd already found the first clue on the back of that photo. She decided to look into it the next morning, and then she'd make a loaf of her honey oat bread and finish the weeding.

"It's miraculous – the amount you get down. I hope I'm as lively at your age," her next-door neighbour would say.

"You have no idea," she'd think to herself, and then with a smile, she'd offer them some of her best batch of bread.

# <u>Letters across the Atlantic</u>

Write an epistolary story set during a major historical event.

The event may be the subject of the letters directly, or be

referenced in the background.

1800+ Creative Writing Prompts To Inspire You Right Now (reedsy.com)

Dear Mummy,

I'm writing like I promised I would. God knows how many weeks it'll take for this letter to reach you. It took two months to get here on the boat. It wasn't what I'd imagined. Did you know they call them Coffin Boats? A fifth of the passengers on board died of Yellow Fever. I was one of the lucky ones, I think. This land of opportunity isn't exactly what I thought it would be. We didn't get a glorious fanfare of a welcome when we stepped off the boat. In fact, I could feel the contempt of those that met us as we first got off the boat. It was a passage of survival. We got to New York after weeks of seasickness and death. I had to sleep in a bunk with several strangers. We tried to comfort each other with anecdotes but hearing them talking about their own experiences just made me homesick. The smell on board was foul, but there was no escaping it. It's not a journey I'd ever wish to repeat. I doubt I'll ever get the chance to return home in person. I have to make a life for myself here, but it's hard to know where to start whenever you have nothing.

I'm sorry for complaining. I know you have it much harder at home. I hope you're still alive and healthy. How are Lily and Bobby? I hope they're helping you around the house. I know

Aoife's death shook everybody. I've been thinking about you every minute of every day and worrying about your poor empty tummies. I hope the blight ends after this crop. It feels like it's bound to. Two bad crops are enough for anyone to bear. The food here is bountiful, but everything costs money. I'm working hard for my wages and for the little room I'm renting. The lady I rent from is tough, but she's kind-hearted. Sometimes she brings me dinner when she has leftovers. It's hard to get used to the food here. I've been living on rice and beans, and I'm grateful for every bite I get. I know how precious it is.

I'll never forget about you for a minute, no matter how busy I get here. It's lonely, but I know I'm lucky to be here. Few people got the chance to come to America, or if they did, they didn't make it off the boat. I'll be praying for you all, and I hope you can write soon to tell me about what's happening at home.

Love,

Ellie.


Dear Ellie,

Don't worry about sharing your woes, love. You've had a long, tiring journey, and I'm sure it was difficult on your own. I heard the boats are dirty and filled with rats. I know it's worth it to get you out of here. There's nothing here for you. You had no opportunities here. Bobby and Lily would probably love to go too, but you know we could only afford the one ticket. I know you'll make the best of it but it's not easy leaving your family behind. We might be stuck with this terrible blight, but we have each other. You're in a country none of us have ever seen and we probably never will, but we can hear all your exciting stories and share your letters together. That will get us through the dark days to come. I'm hoping the worst is over for us now. The stench of the potatoes is still hanging over the house and the fields, but we've grown used to it. We've planted lots of new crops and England have sent us cornmeal in the meantime. It's given us upset tummies, but it's better than the hunger pangs. You know that firsthand. It's strange with your bedroom emptied of your possessions. I remind myself it's different than Aoife leaving because I know you're safe and well. Keep writing to me often to tell me about your new experiences. It heartens all of us to hear that you have a bright future, even if it's tough at the beginning. Have you made any friends yet? Tell me more about the boat and your journey there. What is New York like? I'm dying to hear. I've never seen pictures of it. I don't know anyone that has travelled so far from home before. Is it very different?

Sending you all our love and missing you every day. Write again soon, love.

Mummy


Dear Mummy,

It must have taken weeks for my letter to arrive. I still can't fathom the distance between us. I tell myself it's only one sea, but it still feels so far. I long to hear your voice. It feels like I'm starting to forget it. I've got so used to these American accents. My own voice sounds strange whenever I speak out loud. I found a more permanent job. I was doing odds and ends before now – sewing and washing and whatever I could get. Now I'm working as a maid for a family. It's easier work than what I was doing, and they've given me a room to stay in in their big three-storey house. The houses are different here. No stone or red brick; they're all wooden with painted panels and steps leading up to the porches. People sit on their porches and read or sew or just pass the time talking to their neighbours. It has a friendly feel. The weather is better too. It gets hot in the summer, I'm told, but it's still Springtime here. I'm missing the rain; isn't that odd? We always said it never stopped raining at home, like that was a bad thing. The ground looks yellower here; it isn't as green and the fields are filled with different crops, like sheaves of corn. It's a place of plenty, but you need money in order to have plenty. It's hard for lots of people. I've heard many of the immigrants haven't found work, and some haven't received a welcome. They'd rather keep us off their soil, as far as I can tell. I've heard people talking about the Irish and how poor and dirty they look. It's hard to arrive looking lively after such a gruelling trip. Many had to be put in quarantine whenever they arrived, because of the diseases on board the ships.

Mrs Davis is very kind to me. She got me some new clothes that used to belong to her niece. She said she didn't need them so I might as well have them. It feels good not to wear rags. I am sending money home with this letter. I know you need it more than I do and I'm happy to send it. It makes me feel like I'm helping out in whatever small way I can. I know we agreed that I would come here, but sometimes it feels unfair that I'm living the life I am while you all suffer at home. Even though the potato blight changed everything, I still feel homesick. People eat spuds here, but they aren't as much of a staple. Whenever we have them for dinner, it makes me lose my appetite. I don't tend to talk about home, so no one understands. I can still smell the potato blight even from thousands of miles away. It's a smell that will never leave me, I think, no matter how long I'm here. It's the smell of sickness and death and it haunts me.

I'm glad you are all safe and I hope things are getting easier. Use the money to get as much food as you can. I want to know you're well fed and that you have a better chance to avoid sickness. I wish I'd come here sooner and maybe I could have saved Aoife. If she'd had the food she needed, do you think she still would have died? I wrestle with that thought every day, Mummy. I know it isn't fair to bring it up to you. I know it's harder for you than it is for the rest of us. How are you coping now?

Tell Lily and Bobby I miss them too. I miss you most, Mummy. I'd never been away from you for a day in my life, and now it looks like I'll be separated from you for the rest of mine. Thinking about you all being well keeps me going every day. I still say the same prayers you taught me every night. Whenever I do, it helps to bring back the sound of your voice. God bless,

Ellie


Dear Ellie,

It's Lily. I know you were expecting to hear from Mummy, but she isn't well enough to write. She's got fever and she's tucked up in bed. She's been there since just after she sent her last letter. She got smallpox. I don't know how she got it and how we've escaped it – so far anyway. They say it's an airborne illness, but we barely see anyone anymore. So many people have stopped visiting. I think they're scared of getting sick. There's so much sickness. I just wish it would end. When the new crops come through, we will be alright, and we won't rely so heavily on spuds anymore. I just hope our family makes it through. Losing Aoife was hard enough, and I don't think Mummy could cope with losing another one of us. Since Daddy died when we were little, she's had so much to contend with. It's too much for one woman, but you know how strong Mummy is.

On a happier note, we have been working hard in the garden. We bought lots of seeds and food with your money. It'll keep us going for a while now. We were all painfully thin, but I think we are fattening up and starting to get a healthier glow in our cheeks. We shared what we could with the neighbours; you know Mummy, she always wants to share with others, however little she has herself. You've given us a project and we have been working on the land while Bobby tries to bring home some money too. He's just been working as a farmhand on the local farm, even though there's barely anything left to do there. I don't know how we've made it this far, but somehow, we have. The word of the Lord has helped us all. If we didn't have that, I don't know what would keep us going. We know we need to survive the hard times to reach God's glory.

I have so many questions to ask you about New York. What is it like? Is it as wonderful as everyone says it is? Are the people different than at home? What does it look like there? Do the people talk differently? I've never met an American, but I've heard they have a drawl. Have you been going to church? Mummy hasn't been able to go the last few weeks and it has caused her a lot of upset. You know how much of a devout Christian she is. I don't think she ever missed a service before this. I just wish our prayers were answered a little faster. I'm praying constantly for Mummy. We hope she'll recover after some bedrest and that she'll get outside again. The lack of fresh air can't be good for her. She's too weak to do any household tasks, and you know she likes to be busy. I wish I could cure her, but the doctor can't do anything about it either. He just told us to pray hard. That's all any of us can do for her.

After all this is over, I hope that I can join you in the city one day. I know we don't have the funds for it now, but maybe one day we will. Times of trouble are always followed by times of prosperity.

Wishing you all the best and missing you every day. Please write again soon.

Your sister,

Lily

Dear Lily,

How is Mummy now? I've been desperately awaiting your response. I wish we could make the post travel faster. I just want to hear her voice and to hear that she's feeling well again. What way is she? Has she still been confined to her bed? Is she able to do anything yet? I know it's an awful illness and I wouldn't wish it on anyone. It's terrible to hear that she's caught it. I know she'll be ok though. She's so strong. She's always ok. If she isn't ok, how can any of the rest of us manage?

I'm slowly getting used to New York. It feels like such a long time since I've seen any of you. I miss you every day too. Tell me what you and Bobby have been doing? Is he enjoying working on the farm? Do you have to do all the chores alone now? I'm sure you're taking great care of Mummy. Did the doctor visit again? Sorry you're getting a barrage of questions, but I have so many to ask you too.

It is very different here. The weather is warmer, and the architecture is funny. Everything is much fancier than the farmhouses and cottages back home. The houses are so big, they could hold twenty people, but there are normal sized families living in them - in the neighbourhood I'm working in, at least. I'm getting a glimpse of what it's like to be rich. Even working as a maid feels self-indulgent. I think about you all back home and I feel guilty that I've got the chance to start over. I feel guilty that I'm not more grateful for it sometimes too. I get homesick, and I cry myself to sleep most nights, just thinking of home and all the silly things I miss. I miss the familiar trees in the garden, the cosy rooms of the cottage and hearing the laughter of those I love. It's silent at night whenever I got to sleep. I miss lying awake, chatting to you about everything we thought our lives would become.

What do you miss from before the famine? I can hardly remember those days now. Do you allow yourself to think about them? We were all so carefree then. Sometimes I wish I could go back there and appreciate everything we had so much more.

Please write to me soon to tell me how Mummy is. I'm enclosing some of this week's earnings to help you get more seeds. I'm glad that's keeping you busy.

Love,

Ellie

Dear Ellie,

I hate to have to write this letter to you. We are still struggling to process it. Mummy passed away a few weeks ago. She looked like she was getting better, but then she took a turn for the worse. I wish she could have got to hug you one last time. I'm sorry to be the bearer of such sad news and by letter, no less.

They took the body away. It's in the local burial ground with so many others. She doesn't even have her own plot. She wouldn't have expected that in the midst of everything that's happening, but I wish she had got the send-off she deserved. She was still so young and full of life. That illness robbed us of so much.

Bobby and I have been getting on with the work that needs to be done. We are just going through the motions, keeping each other alive. I wish we could see you and that you could have had a last conversation with Mummy. I'm sure this news with overshadow anything else I could think to write about, so I'll keep it short.

Keep in touch with us and let us know how you're coping. Bobby is still working hard at the farm, and I have a million things to do at home. Our work seems like it will never be done, but it keeps us going too. We are trying to think positively about the future, but with our recent news, it's tough to do that. Please keep praying for us as we will for you.

All my love,

Lily

# *Untouchable*

Start or end your story with a character receiving a hug or words of comfort.

**1800+ Creative Writing Prompts To Inspire You Right Now (reedsy.com)**

I haven't been touched in five years. I can't remember what it feels like anymore. My life has become so robotic; it's hard to tell what I'm feeling anymore. My husband told me he was a good man. That should have been the first cause for alarm bells, but I took him at his word. I trusted him from the minute we met, because why wouldn't I? I had never met someone of his calibre before.

Coexistence is hard when someone dehumanises you daily. I walk into the same room as him at breakfast time. He gets up before me – to avoid me, I think. He makes himself toast and coffee and sits in his favourite chair. I'm not allowed to use it. I hear the crunch of his teeth on the toast and loud sips of coffee – the signal of the commencement of another bad day. There have been so many, they are innumerable. After taking his time over his breakfast, he gets up from his seat, leaving the cushions crushed and the seat misshapen from his substantial mass. I come downstairs like a dormouse, timid with every step. I don't dare to make myself a noisy breakfast. I quietly prepare something to satiate my appetite and I sit on my own seat – hard and unforgiving – eating as quietly as I can muster. We don't exchange a word throughout this entire performance. I glance at him, but only whenever he is looking elsewhere. He looks like an angered bull, ready to charge if I misspeak. I try to keep my distance, even though the last thing I need is distance. I crave human closeness, but not from him. He's my prison guard, policing my cell, day and night. We do this daily dance, but it isn't a joyful one. I used to like dancing, outside in the rain. I listened to my Walkman, whenever they were still in use, decades before my marriage. I used to walk barefoot in the grass of my garden, dancing to my own tune, feeling as free as a water lily. Not anymore. That person is a stranger to me now. Whenever I look at myself in the mirror, I don't know who I am. I just know my face looks worn and exhausted. I barely have the will to repeat another day. That's all it is: repetition. Each day is identical to the last, lacking the emotions that make a life worth living.

I set about my chores for the day. I have a mountain of laundry to do, and the place looks like a dumping ground even though I had it sparkling the previous day. I'm not allowed to get a regular job but that's fine because I have a huge workload to get through each day anyway. I wouldn't have a hope of getting it done if I had to go out to work too. I suppose he's doing me a favour, in a twisted way. He goes out to work each day, as a builder. He comes home whenever he decides to. His work is usually followed by a trip to the pub.

Sadly, he's in a worse mood after he's had a drink. But it's the difference between six and half a dozen eggs, in the end of the day.

I scrub the life out of the floor, on my hands and knees. He says he wants to be able to see himself in it, and he does check. It's strange though, because he is an incredibly untidy person and he systematically works his way around the house, undoing everything I've done after the inspection's over.

He wasn't always like this. He used to have a good heart, by appearances, at least. I can vaguely remember the way he wooed me. The flowers he gave me that turned to dust long ago, returning to the earth like I will at the end of this suffering-filled life. It's all a distant dream, so far in the past that I can only recall pieces of the story. I like to tell myself that that person is still in that body. He's just well hidden beneath the persona he likes to put on at home. If I stopped telling myself that narrative, I'd have to leave, and that's too much to think about. I can't even begin to think about how I would disentangle my life from his. We are enmeshed: in our finances, our home, our reliance on each other.

Sometimes whenever he is asleep, I get up after midnight and go and gaze at the stars and moon brightly glowing in the sky.

They seem so far away but I can graze them with my fingertips through the window. It's like I can almost touch a dream of something else, if only I had the bravery to step out from behind the glass. But that's what frightens me: what if it's an optical illusion? What if, on the other side of the glass, I find out that they're unreachable and then it's too late to turn back? I know if I ever dared to leave our home, the door would be forever locked to me. That's why I never do. I don't know how I would begin to live without him giving me my life force anyway. I don't remember what I used to think before we met, when I had independent thought and I was incapable of looking after myself, or anything else. He has strengthened me, in a way, even if it's been done by means of bullying, over the course of years, decades, a lifetime.

One day, I had to go out on my own, and he let me go. It was for a gynaecological examination. That kind of thing makes him uncomfortable. He told me to attend to my "female troubles" and then to hurry home. Whenever I walked into the doctor's office, I felt naked without him by my side. I didn't need to strip down to my underwear to feel that way. The nurse looked at me. She didn't permit me to look away.

"Oh, love, you look like you need a good hug," she said, and before I had time to protest, she wrapped me in her embrace.

It felt weirdly foreign, uncomfortable, like acupuncture. I might have needed it, but I'd forgotten how to want it. After the appointment was over, I hurried home; back to the safety of being untouched.

# *Saturday, Again*

It's the last evening of your vacation and you're watching the

sunset with your friends/partner/family, wishing summer

would never end. But just as the sun dips below the horizon,

you notice it returning in reverse.

1800+ Creative Writing Prompts To Inspire You Right Now (reedsy.com)

Saturday's sunset was spectacular. Every one of us was sad to see it going to sleep, but its departure was a beauty that only the sky could produce. We looked at one another, knowing that we were sharing that bittersweet ending to our holiday. We had to fly home the next day and none of us wanted to. We were in Lake Garda and the weather had been glorious. We'd lounged by the pool in surroundings that bordered on the divine, and the following day, we had no choice but to go back to the dull, dark UK. Remote weather-watching told us that rain awaited us upon our return.

Endings are always sad, no matter how much you have anticipated them, but they're so much worse whenever you've been dreading them since the very beginning. I knew from the moment we touched down on Italian soil that I wouldn't want to leave. We'd been spoilt over the two-week period we'd spent there. We were treated like royalty by the hotel we'd been staying in. We hadn't had to lift a finger, unless it was for something pleasurable, like going for a swim. The head of the sun was vanishing over the horizon, and then it was gone; until it bounced back again. It reared its head over the horizon again in a moment so foreign I had the impression the world must be ending. Nothing else could explain such a phenomenon.

At first, I thought I was hallucinating; not in the conventional sense, but I thought I was seeing what I wanted to see. Your mind is capable of creating the most improbable things whenever it is desperate enough to see them. But no – the rest of my group started to gasp and then to scream. It was horrifying, even though it amazed us. You can witness the most beautiful sight on Earth, but if it's unnatural to you, it can still leave you with a feeling of horror.

The sun continued to rise, until the round fireball was wholly visible again. Joshua kept using God's name in vain. The others were either silent or screaming; the two most common reactions to shock. Isabelle looked into my eyes, deeper than she ever had before. "What?" she mouthed at me, as if I could know the answer. I couldn't think of a thing to say to her. I almost expected the world to end that second. Wasn't that the type of thing that came right before the apocalypse?

The sun was moving upwards. We were frozen in time, and I had no sense of how long we'd been watching it for. I knew it was moving at the typical speed of a sunrise, but I couldn't take my eyes away from it. I'd never watched a sunrise so closely before. It's funny the things you take for granted whenever you know they happen every day. We were witnessing a once in a lifetime event – whether it ended in our demise or not. It was one of those news-worthy moments we'd be interviewed about later, if we even survived it.

We started to talk in reverse - each word we'd spoken before the sun had set but arranged into inverted sentences. I couldn't stop myself, no matter what I did. Cole had a coughing fit that he'd had moments before sunset. He'd choked on nothing, and we'd all laughed about it, but the laughter came before the cough this time. We were acting in ways that felt like they'd already been coded into time. We had no control over our actions. We were doing it all over again, but in reverse.

The sun was climbing while we talked. Maybe if you will something to happen enough, it can come into being. I'd wished all day long that Saturday would never end, that we could redo the whole thing – and here we were. It wasn't exactly what I'd had in mind. If we could stall time, would we? That's an important question to ask ourselves. In theory, yes, but was the reality of it different? I tried to ponder that, but it was hard to allow space for my own thoughts when we were acting everything out again, back to front. Isabelle was talking about the sunset, but with jumbled words, it was hard to make sense of what she was saying, even though I'd heard it all before. Her regret echoed over the quiet Italian sunset (that was really a sunrise.) The sky was gradually lightening, and the sun was returning to its uppermost point. It would take hours to get there, but I could see where it was going. It was all becoming completely predictable. The day in reverse was different than it had been the first time around. We got to our feet and walked back towards the hotel, away from our viewpoint.

Isabelle was talking about how full she was. "full so am I," she said. "?much so eat I did How"

"?do to meant you are else What .buffet eat can you all an It's" answered Cole.

Trying to reorder the words, to make them make sense, to find out that we'd already heard them a couple of hours earlier, was disappointing work.

I thought I'd give anything on Earth to have that indescribably perfect day all over again, and it had landed in my lap, like a wish from a genie's lamp, delivered in a way that could never live up to the original version. I was angry with myself for ever entertaining the idea that it could. The allure of the unknown was tempting me, even if it meant going back to the greyness of the UK. The weather might have been predictable there, but at least nothing else was. I wondered if it was some sort of test – to make me realise what I'd had before I wished the future away; like a moral lesson provided by a preachy children's book. But I didn't have the key to return to normality. Was it just a lesson in the power of the present, or was it science fiction? Only time would tell.

# Dabbling with the Devil

Write a story about someone making a deal with the devil.

1800+ Creative Writing Prompts To Inspire You Right Now (reedsy.com)

Satan's smiling at me. I don't know why I'm shocked to see him; I invited him here. He looks much more alluring than I could have imagined. He doesn't have any horns, nor is he red with a pitchfork. He looks like a pleasant man: good looking and friendly but with eyes that are hypnotically evil. He reminds me of a serial killer I've seen in a documentary – one of the affable ones you couldn't help but like, despite knowing the monstrosities of which they are capable. He is easy to talk to, welcoming, cheery – everything that no one expects him to be.

He stands over me in my house. He is tall and his presence is commanding, but he waits for me to offer him a seat. He acts polite and self-effacing, but he sits down with the authority with which a king sinks into a throne. I wait for him to speak first. I might have summoned him, but I don't know what to do after that. He has a stench I can't stand. It's like burnt rubber. You can tell he's been in close contact with fire. I try not to focus on it, but it's overpowering. It assaults my senses, but he doesn't seem ashamed of it.

"What can I do for you, Richard? Why did you call me here?"

He must already know, but he plays dumb. He wants me to say it – to beg for his help. I just have to relinquish my soul in return. I'm ok with that – I've never been much of believer in souls. I just want a comfortable life on Earth, and then, to retire to the soil.

What brings me here, you may wonder? How do I end up having to make a pact with the devil? It's simple; I started to age. I was getting creases in my face that I couldn't hide. I'd been told how youthful I looked for many a decade, but the compliments had ceased. I knew I looked my age, if not older. Stress shows on the face, and I'm guilty of stressing over the smallest things. My mum always warned me if I pulled an ugly face it would stay like that, and she was right in the end. My jowly appearance was bothering me day and night. It might seem like a superficial problem, but it isn't, and I'll explain why. I'd fallen in love with a younger woman. I'm in my fifties, and she is only in her twenties. I can tell she has feelings for me, but she'd probably never act on them with me at this age.

I'm a university lecturer. Funnily enough, I teach nineteenth century French poetry and I'm always writing about the evil side of life. "Les fleurs du mal" (the flowers of evil) has always been my favourite poetry collection, but I never considered it to be something that could touch me outside my academic life. People think I'm in a position of power, but I have no power over my own destiny. That was why I called in Satan to help me. I'd spent an evening reading old horror by candlelight and it had put me into the right frame of mind for calling in the devil. It was like using a Ouija board; you didn't know what would happen until you started playing around with it. The reality had exceeded my non-existent expectations.

I thought of the woman I loved. She was a student of mine, but over the age of consent. She'd always been mature for her age. She was in her final year. I hadn't ever crossed the line with her, but I could feel the connection between us. I knew she must have felt it too, but my worn, tired face was a barrier between us. She probably viewed me as a father figure, and that wasn't what I wanted. I just needed youth to return to me and give me the chance to be considered a romantic possibility. She was going to be an academic too. I'd predicted it from day one when she entered my lecture theatre. She hadn't even sat close to the front, but I had noticed her right away, like sunlight beaming through an entwined, matted covering, and somehow prevailing. The rest of the students fitted into a certain stereotype, but she was special. She was a potential PhD student; I could feel it. She'd probably remain in the university for the duration of her career, and I would be forced to be in her company each week, quietly suffering.

The devil smirked at me. "I already know what you want from me," he said. "It's obvious how you feel about Clare."

"I just look so old," I said. "I feel it too. I feel it in my bones, and I feel it any time I look in the mirror."

"I can help you. You'll feel like you're twenty again. There's just the small matter of the exchange."

"The exchange?"

"I give you what you want, and you give me your soul in return."

"Yes, I'm aware of that. It's a fair exchange," I said. Had I known the consequences, maybe I wouldn't have been as quick to agree. Ignorance is ecstasy when it comes to having dealings with Satan.

He stared into my eyes with such intensity I felt like I was being swallowed whole by him. I was no longer a being with free will. I could feel a huge emotional shift even though I was still in the same body.

"I'll give you everything you want. Just be loyal and return your side of the bargain," he said, severely.

He got to his feet, and he seemed to glide across the floor and then vanished into the ether. It felt like I could have dreamt it, but I knew in my gut that I hadn't. I felt like a changed person, just from being in his presence for a short time. I felt contaminated and there was no backtracking. I had to stay committed to our agreement. He had the power to punish me in unimaginable ways.

The next time I saw Clare, I wondered if it had all been worth it. I was in my body from thirty years earlier. Everything felt physically better. I had my full head of hair, my nails weren't yellowed, my teeth weren't stained, the lines in my face were smoothed out. Whenever I looked into the mirror, I was happy with the reflection I saw, externally. But inside, I felt terrible. I shook it off and reminded myself of my realised dream. As soon as I started talking to Clare, I could feel her attraction to me. Strangely, she didn't treat me any differently – she didn't even mention the change. It was like I had always been that way. She was making moves towards me – a touch of my arm here, a kiss on the cheek there. I'd got what I wanted: the woman that I was desperate to be with.

But I wondered if the strength of my feelings had come from my longing, rather than my desire for her. Now that she was available to me, it felt different. She didn't look as perfect up close as she had done with the age difference between us. I could see her flaws and I felt a sinking feeling in my stomach.

I'd sacrificed my soul: something I thought meant nothing, for something that was merely fleeting.

Clare smiled at me and pressed her hand into mine. She didn't know what I was thinking, and she never would. We'd never be real with each other, and it turned out that that was all that mattered in the end. I couldn't even thank the devil for what he'd done for me. I'd been tricked. He'd played me and I'd allowed myself to be played because of a fancy. My soul was forever his, and it was all for nothing. It was the first day of an eternity of bad days.

# A Haunting to your Health

Set your story in a creepy mansion — except nothing horrifying takes place in it.

1800+ Creative Writing Prompts To Inspire You Right Now (reedsy.com)

"It's the most haunted house in the country," said Orla.

I could instantly feel a shudder of fear travelling through me. My body felt as cold as unbreakable ice shards. I didn't want to go there. I was always afraid of the spiritual world. I tried my best to back out of it, but Orla wasn't having it.

"Christa, you have to come. It's for you. I can't tell you the details, but you just have to be there."

I didn't know why she needed me there. If she wanted to put herself in harm's way, why did I have to tag along? I couldn't think of a get-out clause, so I ended up standing next to her on the night of our arrival, dread filling me as I stared at the solid oak door. It looked as sturdy as the entrance to a medieval castle. Once we entered, I knew it would be next to impossible to get out again, but I had no choice but to follow her. I felt compelled to do what she told me to. It was like there was a spell cast over me before I even walked through the door. The power of the atmosphere chilled me to my bones. The air felt like the iciest of handshakes.

Christa walked in like she owned the place. She didn't look the least bit hesitant. Her bravery was much more impressive than mine. She'd made contact with the dead before. As a paranormal investigator, her intrigue overtook any fear she might have felt. I let her lead the way. It was already dark – a storybook Winter afternoon. It was one of those days where the sun only makes a brief appearance before setting again. It was fear-inspiring, and the house didn't have any artificial lighting to counteract it. We had an ample supply of candles, but they didn't illuminate every corner in the way I hoped they would. It felt like areas of the house were enshrouded in darkness to the point that we couldn't know what was lurking there.

The two of us were like two dust mites carried by a strong breeze. We didn't have any way of protecting ourselves from whatever might come. I knew something terrible was going to happen. I didn't know what would befall us, but I sensed it would be destructive in an irreversible way.

Christa smiled at me, "Would you lighten up?" she teased. "You look as tense as I do when I'm at the gym."

"I must be bad," I joked back, but I could feel my body trembling.

I was shivering without restraint, my teeth practically chattering together. I felt like a clichéd horror character. It was only a matter of moments until something happened to me. I'd probably be the supporting friend that got killed off in the first act. I was discovering my own timidity, and it was disappointing to acknowledge it.

Christa opened a set of double doors and we walked into what looked like a ballroom. *Cluedo* was all I could think of. The setting was exactly like that. I just hoped I wouldn't be bludgeoned with a candlestick in the coming minutes.

"Relax," Christa said, with exasperation. "Just try and enjoy yourself."

I wondered what there was to enjoy. I couldn't see past my own fear to consider feeling any other sensations. The windows were covered in thick drapes made of burgundy velvet. They blocked out the outdoors like theatre curtains. It made you wonder what scene could be set up behind them. A whole world could have existed there – a world that usually only featured in nightmares. The furniture was a deep mahogany with embroidered cushions and detail upon detailed detail. It was regal, but not in a way that drew envy from me. I wished I was happily seated in my modern-day flat, small though it was, sipping kettle-boiled water in the spotlight-lit kitchen. I would have exchanged the atmospheric tension for bland peace any day of the week.

The walls were covered in dusky rose wallpaper. They were so faded that I didn't imagine they ever could have livened up the room. I knew the place we were in was vast. One room could have housed my entire flat and there were a multitude of others. I didn't know what the plan for the evening ahead was, and I still couldn't read Christa's mind. I'd never been able to do that. It didn't matter how long we'd known each other for. She was an enigma. It was characteristic of her: the fact we were there at all. I perched on the edge of a fabric covered seat. It brought a whole new meaning to the word "discomfort." I looked at all the knickknacks that were peppered throughout the room. The vases looked like urns. They had the typical period print on them and the gold rims. They weren't pretty, even though they tried to be. There wasn't an object there that I didn't associate with the deceased.

There was a grand piano sitting to the side of the room. The sheet music was propped up on the stand and it rustled in the draught. I could imagine a ghostly figure seated there, playing classical staples, their fingertips barely glazing the keys. I could hear the mournful melody without it being played. Maybe that was what it meant for a place to be truly haunted: your mind started to play tricks on you, and you couldn't pinpoint what was at the root of it all: if it was you or the house.

The door creaked like a coffin lid opening; one that had been shut long ago, one that had been presumed sealed forever. I felt the hairs on my skin standing as straight as sewing needles. The door made an ugly groan, and everyone flooded in; all my best friends were standing in the doorway, smiling.

"We thought you'd like a touch of luxury for your big night," a familiar voice said. It somehow sounded foreign in that strange room. "Congrats on the new job."

Christa blew the dust off the wine glasses in her hand and poured the blood-like fluid into each one. She distributed them, one by one, so we could all sing "cheers;" so we could all relax and have a merry evening.

# No Michelin Star Here

'The worst meal I've ever tasted.' Imagine a zero-star

TripAdvisor restaurant review: capture the customer's

evening out that compelled them to complain

1800+ Creative Writing Prompts To Inspire You Right Now (reedsy.com)

If I could give it zero stars I would. The funny thing is the name of the restaurant should have been a warning in itself. It was called the Michelin Star Inn. It didn't really have a Michelin star; that false claim was just a cheap marketing ploy. I wonder on reflection if any inns have Michelin stars. They're too homey for fine dining, but still, I fell for it. That makes me feel idiotic, knowing that their laughable promotional idea worked on me. I thought I was reasonably intelligent, but I've questioned my own brain power since that day.

I walked inside and there was nothing immediately alarming in the surroundings. First impressions can be misleading. They'd hidden a lot of dirt in the dark corners, pretty lights distracting your eyes, so you didn't get acquainted with them until you were already sitting down - and you'd committed yourself to seeing the meal through.

I was seated at a table beside the toilets. No one hopes to eat in a location where urinary and faecal movements are audible through the neighbouring door. My stomach isn't easily turned, so I didn't bother asking to be relocated. I thought if I overlooked it, the meal would make up it. Their menu was overloaded with options. They used print so small you would have required an eyeglass to see it. I wondered how one kitchen could possibly produce such an array of different meals. Had I given it more thought, I might have walked out then and there, but sadly, I sat on.

My posterior was offended by the uncovered seats. They were made of hard wood, like bar barrels: somewhere designed for perching rather than getting comfortable for the duration of a meal. Still, I didn't complain. I knew they were trying to create a certain "feel" to the place. It was convincing as an 1800's era inn. I noticed there were a dangerous number of candles close to the exposed wood. I didn't know if they were there to create ambience or to keep the electric bill down. In hindsight, I think it must have been the latter. They might have been an unsuitable replacement for heating too.

The waitress approached us, with a worried look, like she was holding her hand out to a rabid dog. She hoped I'd give her a friendly lick rather than tearing off a limb. Maybe she was used to that. Maybe she had good reason to be used to it. She didn't greet us or ask if I'd had time to look at the menu. She rattled off the specials like she was a child, unwillingly reciting her spellings to her mother. It didn't inspire me to try any of the daily offers. There was monkfish on the menu, but I knew it would be tough. Never get seafood when you're too far away from the sea, I say.

My stomach was complaining by then. I'd already been there for the length of a slowly eaten meal, and I hadn't even ordered yet, nor did I feel compelled to order anything in particular. So, I went for the mixed grill. It is hard to get wrong and you are guaranteed a good-sized portion, in my experience. By the time the meal finally appeared, I was considering what I was going to do with my pension, and I'm only thirty-five years old.

I expected it to be piping hot, at least. I could almost forgive a poorly cooked meal if it arrived at a hot temperature, but it was lukewarm. I didn't bother to alert the waitress to the fact because she had such a bored expression, I knew that sharing anything resembling a complaint would be met with nothing but lethargy. I knew she'd just remove the plate and I mightn't see another one, if I was lucky. I don't know which is worse: a bad meal or no meal at all.

I prodded the mushroom with my fork. It looked like it was sweating butter all over the plate, and not in a good way. There was a grey juice coating everything else on the plate. The meat was overcooked. I had a steak knife, but I needed a hacksaw. No, scratch that – a chainsaw. My side of chips was substandard too. They were so pale I wondered if they'd even been introduced to the oil that night.

It was all extremely disappointing; so disappointing, in fact, that I didn't order dessert. To a glutton like me, that's like refusing cake on your own wedding day. I deserved it, but I didn't think my belly deserved to suffer any further. You know a meal has been bad when you find yourself fantasising about your own home cooking instead, and I'm no chef.

I wasn't asked if I enjoyed my meal when the waitress removed my plate. It was probably a question the staff had been advised to stop asking. My full plate adequately answered the question anyway. It looked much the same as it had when they'd brought it from the kitchen, but rearranged into a new, but no more unappetising formation.

I knew I wouldn't be leaving a tip. The service was sullen, and that's a kind description of it. The entire meal was interrupted by draughts of air that came from the bang of the bathroom door as people went in and out in a continuous flow. I'd never realised how often people needed to use the bathroom before. I'd never had a reason to take it under my notice, especially not in a restaurant. You don't want to be reminded of your baser bodily functions while your palate is doing its refined job. As I said, I have a stomach of steel and I'm not easily turned off, but this was an experience I have no desire to repeat.

I wonder if there are any real chefs employed in the kitchen, or if it's just a team composed of several stragglers they found on the street. To add insult to injury, they close at nine PM and if you've failed to vacate your table at that hour, they upturn unused chairs onto your table. Has there ever been a clearer way of telling someone to get out? What more can I say. I won't be hurrying back, but if you decide to proceed (at your own risk) after reading this review, remember to bring your own bottle, own food and own plate. Hell, bring your own pots and pans and offer to make it yourself.

# _Pooltime Serenade_

Write a scene in which a character's behavior or reaction to something is affected by a past experience — without saying what that experience was.

1800+ Creative Writing Prompts To Inspire You Right Now (reedsy.com)

Her feet are at the poolside, placed on the very edge, toes primed for the plunge. Her body is a stiff, unwieldy skeletal structure. Her bikini feels like bondage and the unforgiving sun roasts her exposed back. Sara is stuck in limbo – one that exists between the solid and watery worlds. Everyone around her is laughing and squealing, as if they're mocking her fear as she inches forwards. She tries to drown out the sounds, but it is impossible. Everyone is in full-fledged holiday mode, except for her. This is her moment: the one she worried about all year, since she booked the holiday; one week in Palma but one moment by the pool that stretched out interminably. Her sunglasses laze by her side, their legs bowed, the dark lenses doing no service to her eyes. Her vision needs to be crisp and clear, like a hunter's. She needs to see to the bottom of the pool, to outsmart her fear.

Sara is alone. She wants it to be that way. She has friends that jumped at the chance to accompany her to Palma, but she needs to do this alone, to prove to herself that she can. Often, the thought of a dreaded decision is worse than the decision itself, but this is different. Now she is positioned, ready to slip into the shimmering sunlit water, she feels like terror is going to eat her whole. Her legs are treasures. She never takes them for granted for a second. With one hand missing, she knows the true value of her limbs.

Everyone else is jumping in and out of the water without care. Kids are doing cannonballs and screaming as they go. Fun-filled screams and terror-filled ones can be hard to tell apart. They trigger you either way when you've screamed with real terror yourself. Sara knows she looks strange sitting there, lengthily planning her entry into the water. Maybe to others, she just looks like she's relaxing, but she knows that others are watching her out of interest, waiting to see what she'll do. She pictures herself jumping into the water. It's like stepping off a ledge. The net might be there, but you can only when find out if it works when you leap.

The water glistens in the sunshine. The day is perfect, in theory. She knows there has been some extreme weather there, but it has passed now. It is that picture perfect, postcard type of scene: the sun, the beach, the smiling sun worshippers. The heat is oppressive: the dry kind of heat that only the undulations of cool water can relieve. She knows her body wants to feel that relief, so why is it so hard to make the move?

She knows some moves are fatal, and she is lucky her last one wasn't. But do people get to escape twice? Logically, she knows this is a different scenario, but whenever overpowering emotion takes hold, logic sinks straight to the bottom of the pool.

A man comes and sits beside her. "Typical," she thinks. How do strangers sense whenever someone needs to be alone and select that particular moment to move in for the kill? She doesn't need friends there; she needs space to think. She needs to get over this by herself.

"Do you need any help?" he asks, beaming at her.

He is looking at the place where her hand used to be. He is likely thinking of the beauty she could have been without this disfiguration of hers. When he approached her, she might have been a figure of desire, but now, she feels diminished to a figure of pity.

"No, thanks," she says, through gritted teeth. "I'm just having a rest."

"Ok," he says, frowning. "I'll leave you in peace."

She nods. At least he isn't slow on the uptake. She doesn't bother watching him walking away. She can picture it in her head: the drooped head, the look of defeat, but she can't deal with that right now. She needs to stay focused, or her holiday has all been for nothing.

She made a bet with her brother before she left: fifty for her if she got in the water, fifty for him if she didn't. She could have lied. He wasn't there to witness it, so how would he ever know? But her self-respect would know. It would remind her of her perceived failure every day. She has to conquer this demon of hers.

The water does its best to look inviting, and it obviously is to all the other guests. It is that photographic kind of enticing that inspires envy in those that aren't there. It has cost her entire savings to get there, to create the perfect stage for her moment of glory. But she can't jump. She can't slide in either, nor make a gentler approach to the water. Her body cries out for the pool's cooling touch, but her mind isn't to be mastered. She's been there long enough to acquire obvious sunburn, and she knows it is the moment of truth. She moves one single toe forwards and dangles it above the pool water. One more movement and it would be submerged, and it would be over, and she'd be proud of herself. But what if? Her mind can't stop dredging up the "what ifs." She puts her good hand on her ankle to steady her shaking toes, but she can't stop them. They have come into a life of their own. They are like friends that give you a shake when they see you about to destroy your life. They are the kind you trust and listen to because they've always been there for you.

Sara stands up on the hot brickwork. Her feet burn and she knows she needs to get back to her sandals. She tiptoes across the ground, absorbing painful heat with every step. She gathers her towel and her shoes, heading back in the direction of the hotel. She walks around the perimeter of the pool, and then, she pauses at the baby pool. She looks down at the aquamarine blue – a foot of water with visible ground at the bottom, and she thinks, "what if I started here?"

Printed in Great Britain
by Amazon

36785172R00076